All rights reserved. No part of this book may be reproduced in any form by any electronic or mechanical means including photocopying, recording, or information storage and retrieval without permission in writing from the author.

The Missing Father
Paperback Copyright © 2021 Lorhainne Ekelund
Editor: Talia Leduc

All rights reserved.
ISBN-13: 9781989698501

Give feedback on the book at:
lorhainneeckhart@hotmail.com

Twitter: @LEckhart
Facebook: AuthorLorhainneEckhart

Printed in the U.S.A

THE MISSING FATHER

The O'Connells

LORHAINNE ECKHART

About the O'Connells

The O'Connells of Livingston, Montana, are not your typical family. Follow them on their journey to the dark and dangerous side of love in a series of romantic thrillers you won't want to miss. Raised by a single mother after their father's mysterious disappearance eighteen years ago, the six grown siblings live in a small town with all kinds of hidden secrets, lies, and deception. Much like the contemporary family romance series focusing on the Friessens, this romantic suspense series follows the lives of the O'Connell family as each of the siblings searches for love.

The O'Connells

The Neighbor
The Third Call
The Secret Husband
The Quiet Day
The Commitment, An O'Connell Novella
The Missing Father
The Hometown Hero
Justice
The Family Secret
The Fallen O'Connell
The Return of the O'Connells
And The She Was Gone
The Stalker

The O'Connell Family Christmas
The Girl Next Door

―――――――――――――――――

About The Missing Father

―――――――――――――――――

The O'Connell family collides with danger in this shocking new story from *NY Times* and *USA Today* best-selling author Lorhainne Eckhart.

Eighteen years ago, Luke O'Connell's father was there one day, gone the next. His mother sat him and his siblings down and told them their father was gone, it was just them now, and they wouldn't be seeing him again. But Luke never believed his father could just walk away from a family he'd said he loved. Now, from his role within a secretive military organization, he uses the intelligence he can access to follow leads on his father, but each is a dead end.

Luke finds himself endlessly embroiled in deadly missions from secret bases, posing as a civilian for front companies, and tracking national enemies to capture or kill. But now, his questions have brought trouble back with him onto US soil, all the way to his hometown—

and ultimately, his quest might put his family in the line of fire.

———————————————

Chapter 1

———————————————

"So what you're saying is our target is a whistleblower?" said Master Sergeant Rex Barnes. "The man grew a pair and exposed a corrupt billion-dollar lab linked to our government, and our target isn't the company itself but the employee, who has now been named an enemy of the state? Just want to be sure I'm one hundred percent clear, here. This lab has been committing crimes against the public, fabricating crime scenes using DNA of their choosing, all with the blessing of the CIA, and we're saying this is okay? The operation was privately funded, yet now the technology is being sold to every rogue government and criminal, and we're meant to target the whistleblower who exposed the scheme? A man we once would've called a hero is now our enemy? Like, good God, what the hell has become of this country? Have we really been reduced to this?"

Master Sergeant Barnes was dark-haired and blue-eyed, hot-headed and ambitious, and at times he was confused for Luke, considering he had the same long dark hair tied back in a ponytail, the same broad shoulders, and the same height of six feet. Unlike Luke, though, Rex was grandstanding, as he usually did. He still hadn't learned the art of shutting his damn trap and keeping it shut in front of anyone in charge.

"It sounds to me as if you're challenging an order, Master Sergeant," said Colonel Raymond Powers. "Is there a problem here that I don't know about? Because last I heard, how this works is the orders come down from the White House, and you don't question them. It's not up to you to be the judge and jury and decide which assholes you shoot. The order comes down for your mission, I outline it, and you shut the fuck up and follow it. We don't get to question what falls under national security and what doesn't. You're a grunt. You pick up the gun and shoot who we tell you to."

Colonel Powers was the shortest member of the team, in his fifties, a retired operator on his third wife. He was standing at the end of the boardroom table in the command center where they were being briefed, wearing green fatigues and the same pissed-off, unsmiling expression he always had. "Sergeant Major, you need a minute with your team to see they have their heads screwed on straight?" he snapped at Jess Parker, the team leader.

Jess was perched on the end of the table instead of sitting in a seat, and he still hadn't shaved since arriving back stateside three days earlier. His bushy reddish hair was shoulder-length, but his beard and mustache gave him a hillbilly biker look that wouldn't have made him seem out of place on *America's Most Wanted.* Added to that was the tattoo on his forearm, a skull and crossbones emblazoned with the words "Death before dishonor"—something that would've been frowned on in the regular military but was good for their unit.

The 77th Operational Delta, known as the Wardogs, were a special forces team that didn't really exist, reporting directly to the White House, which was both good and bad. It had started because of the war on terror, but, as of late, they had been more focused on protecting the dirty side of business.

"Nope, we're good to go," Jess said. "Seems Barnes has forgotten his manners and how he's supposed to be seen and not heard, just like the child he is, in the presence of his commanding officers. Not to worry. He's figuring it out now that we're back stateside. Isn't that right?"

Jess gave everything to Rex, who only lifted his hands arrogantly and didn't say another word. There was just something about Jess, who'd run their team for six years. He garnered all their respect unconditionally, and he knew how to shut each of them down, take the heat, and keep them all alive.

"So you'll be wheels up in two hours. That will be all," the colonel said before striding out of the secure room on the base at Fort Bragg.

Luke swiveled in the old black leather chair, taking in the now closed door, before turning back toward Sergeant First Class Matthew Newman, sitting across from him in a white T-shirt and khakis. The newbie, at twenty-five, was eager to impress. He was from Nebraska, with hazel eyes and nice, silky, long dirty blond hair and a smile that could sweet-talk the pants off any woman. He could've passed for a surfer, Luke thought, and he always had a different woman on his arm. His eyes could flash with teasing one minute and be filled with the kind of look that would have any sane man running the other way the next.

"I'm with Rex on this one," Matthew said. "This isn't sitting too right, Jess, that someone could use my DNA to fabricate a crime scene while I'm on the other side of the world. Definitely leaves me with a cold chill."

"This is what you signed up for," Jess said. "You're a grunt. You're not paid to think. You follow orders, end of story. The Harris Group is one of the leading genetics companies, responsible for cutting-edge medical research that saves lives." He took in each one of them.

From the other end of the table, Shaun Grant, Sergeant First Class, pitched in. "Doesn't it seem odd to you that we're being asked to go in and shut down this situation before it becomes known to the public? Seems as if more and more, we're becoming hired thugs." His black hair was close cropped, and he had dark skin and dark eyes, the biggest member of the team, at six foot two and likely three hundred pounds of solid muscle. His conference room chair seemed too small for his big frame. To Luke, Shaun was the one they all looked to, who had their backs and was always first through the door.

"So let me get this straight," Rex started again. "We're flying to Switzerland to capture a whistleblower, an executive at a private genetics lab funded by every government worldwide, which is stockpiling DNA from private citizens for all kinds of nefarious means in the name of research and development. He's exposed them for working with the CIA and other countries to manipulate DNA evidence and engineer crime scenes, and he's also exposed our government and the Harris Group for selling their technology to the highest bidder.

"But because he's stepped on the wrong toes and just because our government can, we're supposed to be okay with capturing this poor schmuck? He's the one being screwed here, in my opinion. We're going to toss him away in a hole forever, no trial, no nothing, because he sounded the alarm? This technology could result in any one of us being locked up forever on charges for a crime we didn't commit. Sounds to me like we're on the wrong side of this one."

Luke had long past realized that an order was an order. He'd lost track of the number of missions that had strayed into the corporate world that the government had its hands in. The wrong side was the wrong side, but the lines had started to blur.

"It's not up to us to question it," Jess said, looking around at them. "You know that. We take the order, and you do your job. You don't get an opinion. Are we clear here, or does anyone else have something to get off his chest before we're wheels up?"

To Luke, the five-member team were like his brothers. His family back in Livingston would likely have a serious fit if they knew what really went on behind the scenes in their government, if they knew about the kinds of assholes he was protecting.

"No, fine," Shaun said in his deep voice. "My mama always raised me to believe that honesty is the best policy, but scheming and dishonesty seem to be what we're defending now. Makes perfect sense to me." He was dressed in fatigues and a tan T-shirt. When he swiveled around in his chair, Luke sensed he seemed moodier than usual.

"Great, so now that we're all clear, remember this isn't a sanctioned military operation," Jess said. "We're going in as civilians. Know that this isn't sitting right with me, either, but we don't get to pick and choose our missions. We follow orders. That's what we signed on for. You'll need your suits for this one. Speaking of, Luke, how was your brother's wedding? How's your family?"

Luke could just make out Jess's blue eyes as the man lifted the shades he'd worn inside, something the colonel also never busted him for. But then, they were Jess's team, and they operated under an anonymity that Luke had once appreciated. The things they did wouldn't sit right with members of the regular army.

"He's married, but I'm not sure he buys into it, considering he's still stuck on the fact that our dad ditched us as kids," Luke said. "I didn't know it still bothered him, even though it fucked us all around. But hey, he did it. He's adopting the little girl, too, and I heard before leaving yesterday that he's going to be a baby daddy. Charlotte's preggers."

"Marcus is married, adopting that kid, and now about to be a father? Good for him. I'm happy for him," Rex said, jumping in, all smiles. "Has to make your mom happy."

Luke just took in his team, who'd met his family only a handful of times but knew everything about them and then some. They all knew more about each other and their issues, their secrets, than their own families knew.

Then everyone was up and started to the door, ready to hit their lockers and grab their bags, their guns, everything they'd need.

"Luke, got a second?" Jess added before he could leave.

"Sure," he said, realizing it was only him and Jess left in the conference room.

"Just wanted to give you a heads-up that the lead you asked Sienna to follow up on, the one about Raymond O'Connell, turned up nothing. Yes, Sienna was under the impression that I knew about the request. When she mentioned it to me, I knew the man had to be your dad, and I thought, 'Now, what the hell is Luke doing?' So now I'm asking, why are you having Sienna Parker, our CIA agent, look for your dad?"

In that moment, Luke wanted nothing more than to pull Sienna aside and ask her what the hell she was doing.

"You've known me a long time," Luke said. "Fine, here it is. There's just something about the fact that my father up and walked away from his family eighteen years ago that's never sat right with me. We never heard from him again, and from what I've figured out, he vanished into thin air. Now, who does that? We have the resources, so yeah, I've been doing some homework. You going to bust me for that?"

Jess glanced over to the door and back to him, but he didn't say anything for another second. "Cut the crap, Luke. You can't have Sienna doing personal investigating for you. Your dad evidently doesn't want to be found—but then again, there could be another option."

"You mean that he could be dead?" Luke said. That was the thing he'd thought of over and over. If his father had disappeared and walked away, he was either dead or didn't want to be found. "If he's dead, how is it that I can't find anything on him? The more I dig, the more holes I find."

Jess ran his hand over his chin. "Well, then maybe

you have your answer." He started to the door before turning back to him. "Luke, if you keep digging, the answers you find may not be the ones you want. Oh, and one more thing," Jess said, his hand on the door. "Consider this your birthday present, me coming to you. Sienna's doing you this favor, but then she came to me. You may want to ask yourself, what is she up to?"

Chapter 2

"Hey there, Luke," Sienna said. Her blond hair hung long and loose, and she wore a navy dress and pumps. She was slender and tall, at five foot seven, and she had been working with their team, gathering intelligence, for four years. She was the CIA side, with assets he didn't want to know about.

"Sienna, you're looking rather fetching in that dress," he said.

That was another thing about her: She gave the impression of being a PTA mom, a former cheerleader from the Midwest, but in fact, she was really good at what she did.

She strode up to where he stood in the team's hotel suite on the top floor of the five-star Emperor Hotel in Geneva, where he was cleaning his HK 416. Even though he couldn't carry it under his suit, it was his go-to weapon of choice. However, the spot of sniper on the team was held by Matthew and then Rex. He'd be limited to his Glock today, hidden under his tailored blue suit, and he'd carry a spare strapped to his ankle.

"Ah, thanks, Luke," she said, then shrugged and smiled. "I take it Jess talked to you, letting you know it was a dead end, that Wisconsin lead you had. Sorry about that. I would have told you myself, but I had to hop a plane here for a meeting and thought it seemed urgent."

Bullshit!

He knew by the way she said it. Her hazel eyes, which he couldn't read at times, seemed so noncommittal, and there was something there now that didn't sit right with him. Being straight with the team, with him, was something he expected from her, but whatever this was wasn't straight at all.

"Yeah, about that," he said. "You said you'd do me this favor, checking into someone for me and keeping it on the q.t., but then you went running to Jess with that dead-end nonsense, which we both know is bullshit. When I said this was delicate, sensitive—"

"You mean personal?" she said, cutting him off. She had transformed from friendly and easygoing to unsmiling, in his face. She glanced over her shoulder to where Rex and Matthew were going through their guns and ammo. Luke could hear Jess on the phone, talking, he knew, to the colonel. It would be showtime soon, and he could see something about this still wasn't sitting right with him.

"So what's your deal, Sienna?" Luke said. "We have each other's backs, so I can't figure out why you went to Jess and told him it was a simple dead end when you were all over that lead, wanting to help me when I was searching the database. You said a flag came up on the name I was searching in Wisconsin. You, Sienna, were the one who came to me and asked to check it out for me, so don't give me this crap about it being personal and then blow me off. Everyone here uses the resources we have for personal things, including you, and I made no secret about it.

"I know you, Sienna. You seem to forget I know how good you are, but I also know when you're hiding something, up to something. There's no such thing as a dead end with you. There was something. Seems to me you're hiding it, so I have to ask what it is. You know something. Or is this you trying to jam me up? Who else did you go to?"

He knew he sounded paranoid, but he kept his voice low, wondering what game she was playing.

She slowly crossed her arms, leveling him with a gaze that told him she wasn't taking any shit, appearing very much the image of a woman who was all business. "All right, the name Raymond O'Connell raised a red flag in Wisconsin, a sealed file that even I couldn't get into. I started looking around, and as I'm sure you've already figured out, the Raymond O'Connell you're looking for didn't exist before 1983. Then he suddenly did. He married your mom, Iris O'Connell, and his name is on your birth certificates. He worked for the railroad, seemed to have the perfect, normal all-American life, and then he was gone one day. You also know that no police report or missing persons report was filed. Let me ask you this: You find anything on him from that November day he walked away?"

He just stared at her, sensing that cocky side of her, wondering how she knew everything he did. Evidently, she'd figured out the same things he had.

She looked over her shoulder again and stepped

closer to him. "You ever ask yourself, Luke, how a man can disappear into thin air, without a trace?"

"You mean he was a spook. Is that what you're implying?" he said. He wondered if anyone was listening.

She rested her hand on his arm, a touch that meant nothing to him. She was pretty, not hot, and as single as all of them, considering every one of them had the same screwed-up life that left them far from stable or dependable, without healthy relationships and families.

"Or dead," she said. "That's the more likely scenario that I'm talking about."

"But that wouldn't explain the red flag you said popped up on his name—or the fact that you did blow me off by going to Jess. That has me wondering what you really found out."

"Okay, let's saddle up," Jess announced. "Luke, you, me, and Rex are going to pick up the target, Stefan Schwartz, at the Harris Group. Sienna, you're with Matthew and Shaun at his apartment. The orders are to take his place apart, find everything he has on the company, every trade secret, everything confidential, anything that belongs to the corporation. I want no mistakes. He doesn't know we're coming, so let's get in and get out. Anything you find at his place, tag it, bag it, and pack it up. It goes back to Washington so they can figure out what they're going to do."

The group started to head off. Just as Sienna went to step away, his hand landed on her arm.

"Whoa, we're not done," he said.

Her gaze went right to his hand. She was slender, fit, and he could feel how tense she was. He didn't pull away, but she did. "We are," she said, then took a step in her pumps before turning back to him. "Oh, and no, I wasn't trying to jam you up. Just FYI, the Wisconsin Raymond O'Connell isn't who you're looking for. The flag on the file was from the Feds. The man's in witness protection. They just happened to pick your dad's name."

He let his hand fall away, and Sienna walked off, and Luke didn't miss the fact that Jess was watching all of it.

Chapter 3

"I told you I'm innocent! What do you want from me? Why are you doing this? Where are you taking me? Seriously, I'm not the bad guy here. I didn't do anything wrong. Who are you guys?"

Stefan Schwartz, in his fifties, with graying hair, had been in a board meeting when they walked in with security from the Harris Group. Rex had cuffed him in front of the six other men and women around the table. One had demanded to know what was going on, but they'd been in and out in less than six minutes.

Stefan was now on the floor in the back of the van, cuffed, a hood over his head. There was something about the scene, the fact that they seemed to be serving as corporate security way too much as of late, that wasn't sitting right with Luke.

"Hey, hey! Shut up back there or I'll tape your mouth shut," Jess called out from the passenger seat.

Luke was behind the wheel, and Rex was in back with the guy. He heard something that sounded like duct tape ripping, and he didn't have to look in the rear-view mirror to know that Rex had taped Stefan's mouth. All they could hear was muffled yelling now as they made their way to the airport, mission done. The guy would be on the transport back to Washington that night, and they'd be on a commercial flight the next morning.

Then there was Sienna, whom he wanted to sit down with to find out what was really going on.

"Okay, just heard from Shaun, Matthew, and Sienna," Jess said. "They have everything, and they're already back at the hotel. Said something about a key, encrypted files. Whatever—it's above my paygrade and yours. Can't wait to get back and have a drink. We're done."

He pulled into the airport, up to the military plane that had been waiting. Rex had Stefan out of the back, and he was handed over to military personnel. They were now done. This part of the mission was finished.

"Let's get out of here, get back to the hotel, have a few beers," Rex said as he climbed back into the van.

Luke slid behind the wheel again and took in the military plane, seeing Stefan now shackled as he was led onto it, and for a minute, he sympathized, because he knew the man would never have his day in court. Whatever he'd done or whoever he'd pissed off, he'd stepped on the wrong toes.

They arrived back at the hotel and parked underground, and Luke split off from Rex and Jess as they stepped into the lobby. He took in the glass, the brass, the sofas and chairs, and the front desk as he walked over to the open bar. The place had the same high-end feel as the rest of the hotel. Shaun, Matthew, and Sienna were already sitting there, still in suits, nursing beers.

Shaun was watching everyone, his back to the wall, whereas Matthew seemed almost too cozy with Sienna.

"Hey, there, you made it. First round's on me," Sienna said. She ordered one of the foreign beers for Luke and slid it over to him. "Where're Jess and Rex?"

He leaned against the bar, taking her in, lifting the bottle and gesturing to the bartender in thanks. "They'll be right down," he said.

Jess had to report in, and Rex was likely seeing that their guns were packed down and ready to go, stowed nowhere a maid could see if one walked in.

"So you're heading back to Livingston after we get back to base?" Matthew asked, and Sienna too was watching him as she lifted her gin and soda with a twist of lime. It was the only drink he ever saw her with.

"Yes, after we finish up," he said. "Seems Owen is in a bit of a pickle. Ryan mentioned something about girl trouble. I kind of want to check in and find out what's what with Karen and her hubby, Jack, too. Suzanne seems happy enough, but she got royally screwed over by that asshole Toby, as Marcus put it. Then there's my mom. Didn't get much of a chance to really check in with her."

Shaun lifted his Swiss beer and took a swallow. "Well, at least you have family to go back to."

"Ah, come on, what am I, chopped liver? You know you love spending time with me," Matthew said, moving to put his arm around Shaun, who stepped back, giving him a look as if he should know better.

"You're lucky, Luke, having a family like you do," Sienna said without looking his way.

Luke looked around the bar, seeing corporate types in suits, women in heels, drinking wine and the kinds of expensive drinks that banker types drank. He took in Jess and Rex coming their way and could already hear Shaun ordering their beers.

There was something about Sienna right now. He couldn't shake the feeling that something was completely off, and it bothered him. For the first time, he feared he could be jammed up for something he wouldn't see coming. He didn't want her anywhere near his family or discussing them.

"I am," he said simply, then took in a tall leggy woman at the end of the bar. Her hair was light brown, her face slender, and her dress black. She was holding a glass of white, sitting alone. He couldn't help himself. "You know what?" he said, turning to Jess and Rex, who he knew had also spotted the looker. "I'm going to check out six o'clock down there. Wish me luck."

He picked up his beer and gestured to the bartender. "Bring the woman down there another glass of whatever she's drinking, and bring me another one of these," he said, then made his way down the bar.

Her hazel eyes took him in.

"Well, pardon me, ma'am. Are you with someone?" he said.

The bartender slipped her another glass of white wine, and a second beer for him followed.

"I didn't order this," she said, and her accent, he thought, was French.

The bartender said, "It's from the gentleman."

"Luke O'Connell," he said as the bartender stepped away. "Yes, a little forward on my part, but I spotted you down here alone. You can either tell me to get lost and toss the drink in my face, or you can say thank you and we can share a drink and conversation."

She lifted a brow but didn't smile as she finished off her glass of wine and reached for the other one, sliding it toward herself. She lifted it and took a sip. Something about her seemed flawless. Her dress was classy, with a hint of perfect cleavage, and her fingers were slender and long and ringless.

"Well, thank you," she said, "but I'm not about to waste a perfectly good glass of wine by tossing it in your face. So, Luke. By the accent, I take it you're American." She was confident, and he thought he could listen to the sound of her voice all night.

"Yeah, but I seem to be at a disadvantage here. I've already told you my name, but you've withheld yours. How about we start with introductions?" He held out his hand as he leaned on the bar. "Luke O'Connell, and your name is?"

She slid around on her stool and took him in, holding out her hand. "Rosemary. Nice to meet you. So what brings you to Geneva, Mr. O'Connell?"

"Luke," he said, nearly cutting her off. He wasn't sure what to make of her eyes, the light, the hint of amusement. "Business brings me here." He held her hand, making an exaggerated motion of looking at her ring finger. "I see no ring, so I take it there's no angry mister who's going to show up here and start a bar brawl or shove a fist in my face."

She said nothing for a second. "No, no one." She didn't pull her gaze from him. "And you, Luke, you have a wife hidden at home, a posse of kids, maybe…?"

He just laughed. "No, seems we're the perfect match here, both single in a bar, having a drink. So tell me, Miss Rosemary, are you visiting this beautiful part of the world or do you live here?"

This time, she slid her hand away as she leaned on the bar top, so close that he got an eyeful of her cleavage. "Like you, Luke, I too am visiting."

Chapter 4

Luke ran his hand over his forehead and messy hair as he turned his head into the pillow, taking in the woman beside him in bed. He pulled in a breath, smelling the sweat from another restless night. Sleeping peacefully was just something he didn't do anymore.

He took in his clothes, tossed on the chair by the bed. Light spilled through the window, and he heard a ding from his phone and spotted it in the pocket of his jacket. He slid out of bed and reached for it, then saw the text from Jess.

You still with the babe from the bar? We're leaving. Get your ass back here.

He sent back a quick text, *Be there in a few*, and then slipped his phone back in his jacket, feeling his holstered gun tucked underneath. He heard a rustle from the bed.

She was awake, holding the sheet over her breasts, and he took in the perfection of her face. She had a softness to her. How many drinks had they had? Six or seven, he thought.

"You have to go?" she said. There it was again, something he'd picked up on the night before.

"No French accent, I see," he replied. "So why fake it? What is this, some game?"

It was at drink four when she'd really loosened up and her accent had slipped. He'd said nothing about it then, though of course he'd noticed it. He stepped into his underwear and dress pants, and she pulled her knees up to her chest under the sheets.

He could still picture her every curve, remembering the feel of her soft skin and how he'd run his hands over her. Their kiss had been off the charts, hot and steamy. There had been no hesitation as she slipped her hand in his and took him to her room, which had a king bed and a modest view. Something about her seemed steeped in mystery, in some secret—but then, so was he.

She ran her hand over the back of her neck and looked down and away for a second. Yeah, he'd busted her. He could always tell when someone needed a minute to get on top of a lie.

She gave him everything, taking in his every motion as he pulled on his shirt and re-holstered his gun. She tilted her head. "It's just something I could do, you know, the accent. I've always been good at it. Last night, for me, I felt like playing it up, though I didn't plan on it when you walked over. But since here we are, the morning after, there was nothing honest about you, either. A guy in a bar who makes his way over to a girl with a drink and then keeps buying them for her is only after one thing: sex, nothing more. What difference did it make about the accent? Did you plan on seeing me again? It was just a role I played, and you played one, as well. As you said, Luke, if that's your real name, you're from out of the country, and so am I. We're really just two ships passing in the night, a night of great sex and…" She pulled in a breath. "Anyway, this isn't about me or you. We had some fun, and now you're two steps from the door, so we'll never see each other again."

"I'll have you know my name is Luke," he said. "But let me guess: Yours isn't Rosemary."

She didn't smile. Her hazel eyes told him she wasn't ready to apologize for anything. "Well, actually, Rosemary is my real name. So, Luke, you're from…" She let it hang.

Here it was, where they got into the really personal territory that he wasn't about to share. Despite the sex, they didn't know anything about each other "From Montana. And you, Rosemary, where are you from? From the accent, I'd say Midwest US?"

"Close, or thereabouts. Indiana. So what's with the guns? You're a cop, a criminal, or something else?"

He pulled on his suit jacket, shoved his feet into his shoes, and pulled out his phone. "Not a criminal. I work for the US government. You, what's your number?"

He took in her surprise as he flicked his gaze over to her, phone in hand. What the hell was he doing? He didn't do this, didn't ask for women's numbers, especially not a woman from a one-night stand in another country. But there was something about her, something far from needy and far from typical, something he couldn't shake.

"Why? This was sex, nothing else, no strings, and now you want my number?" She made a rude noise but didn't move to get out of bed, holding the sheet up as if making sure she stayed covered. It was flickering in her eyes, panic or something else, and she stiffened as he watched her. If anything, the way she was acting was almost humorous.

"As you said, there's something about you, Rosemary, once you drop the pretense of being French. Now we're getting down to the nitty-gritty, and we're both Americans, so just maybe I'll call."

He knew he sounded arrogant, and the frown she gave him should have told him he was wasting his time, but instead, what did she do but give him her number? He typed it into his phone and moved around the bed to her. She was brooding, sexy, but he knew nothing about her yet.

"So, Rosemary, what brings you to Geneva, business or pleasure?"

"Luke, seriously, I just gave you my number, but it sounds to me as if you're wanting something more that I'm not looking for. I was willing, remember…?"

He waited, not pulling his gaze, and finally she sighed. Even that sound made him feel things he hadn't expected. Women didn't do this to him, yet this pretty face had gotten under his skin.

"Brooks," she said. "Rosemary Brooks. I do online advertising."

"Well, Miss Rosemary Brooks—and it is 'miss,' right? Since we're getting honest and real right now."

She gave her head a toss, and there it was, a smile. It was the first time that had flickered in her gorgeous eyes. "Unattached, yes. So why does this feel as if you're about to walk out the door with all kinds of promises of calling or getting together? Just so we're clear, I'd just as soon you not. False promises are the worst, you know, sitting around and waiting for a call that never comes. Would you instead like to say thanks for…?" She held out her hand, which he took as he leaned down and pulled her into a kiss, taking it deep, feeling the sheet slip as she went up on her knees, pressing all that softness into him. Then he pulled back.

"Thanks for the night, you mean, for the sex. Well, if I took your number, it means I'll call. But you're right, this was no strings, no nothing. I've got to go, anyway. Have a plane to catch. So tell me, Rosemary, how long are you here in this part of the world?"

She said nothing for a second, and he leaned down and kissed her when she didn't answer. Yeah, there was definitely something there. He pulled back and took in the interest she couldn't hide as she sat back down and reached for the sheet, covering her breasts again. She licked her lips and pulled in another breath.

"Tomorrow I head home," she said.

He stood up and knew he needed to go when he heard his phone ding again. Yeah, Jess would have his ass. She must have known, as she waved her hand.

"Go," she said. "If you call, you call. If you don't, it was nice meeting you."

He started to the door, pulled it open, and looked back at her. "You too, Rosemary," he said, then stepped out, stopping himself from saying he'd call. As much as he'd like it, he was an operator, never in one place long enough to form any type of long-term thing.

He pocketed his phone as he strode to the elevator and pressed the button to take him up to the penthouse, where his team was waiting, and his bags too. It was time to go back home.

Chapter 5

"Just a heads-up, everyone," Jess said as he stood in their warehouse. "Word just came down from Sienna that the raid on the target's condo didn't turn up the missing information, and if it gets into the wrong hands, it could reflect badly on the Harris Group and lead to questions about their partnerships with people in our government who don't want anyone in the public knowing. Apparently, one of the missing documents outlines the terms of the financial aid the group was given by governments, linking them to this DNA fabrication. In the wrong hands, it could embarrass several countries funding this part of the company that isn't supposed to exist. Worse, it could end up in the hands of an enemy who will use it to gain the upper hand."

The safe was open, and Matthew was shoving in several stacks of cash the colonel had handed them when they'd landed. Where exactly it had come from, no one knew for sure. Could've been the treasury or some agency, all unaccounted for. It was something they needed, along with ammunition and guns. Their stash would've been a doomsday prepper's dream, all because they were a part of the government that did the kinds of things that weren't officially sanctioned.

It was their go cash, which they could use to disappear and start a new life in the event shit hit the fan. That was something Luke hadn't considered too closely, because he, unlike the rest of his team, had a family he knew would hunt him down, unwilling to let him go, even if he up and disappeared because he was suddenly on the most-wanted list. His siblings, he realized, could end up on the wrong side of something, asking questions that could end up getting one of them killed.

"Well, maybe that's a good thing," Rex said. "If the White House and these other countries have their hands in this kind of thing, that doesn't sit right. You all know I've voiced my objections quite strongly on this mission. It's one thing when these kinds of genetics companies use technology to find cures for the uncurable, but this little sideline has me wondering about every conviction that has ever been made based on crime-scene DNA evidence. Have entire scenes been fabricated? Seems we really are taking a step into some dangerous territory I'm not entirely comfortable with. If we piss off the wrong person one day, who's to say it won't be our asses on the line, with us being hunted down and set up for something? There's no coming back from that. I mean, who are we taking orders from anymore, anyway? At one time, this war we were fighting made sense."

Matthew closed up the safe, and Shaun was adding their guns to the munitions pile. This commercial warehouse was owned by a numbered company, located in an area that housed everything from retail supplies to automotive shops. No one in the military knew where they set up storage, including their colonel.

"You know something about the missing documents?" Jess said, sitting on a crate in the corner, his arms crossed, his beard and mustache long gone. His hair was short, neat and tidy. Like all of them, Jess was dressed casually in blue jeans and a T-shirt.

"I wish, because if I found them, I'm not sure I'd be too inclined to turn them over to the CIA, who'll likely see them destroyed," Rex said. "No, whatever happened to them, I seriously hope they turn up and shit hits the fan and exposes these assholes."

Luke, like the rest of them, said nothing, and his gaze settled on Shaun, who was lingering in the door.

Matthew stood up. "Well, this has been fun, but not sure what any of that has to do with us. We went in, got the innocent guy, emptied the condo. We're done. Now how about we talk about Luke and the babe he was with? I'd rather hear about that." He was so matter of fact.

"You're just jealous because she wanted me," Luke said. "You had no chance with the babe—whose name is Rosemary, from Indiana, by the way. I even got her number." He didn't know why he'd added that.

"Since when do you ever get a woman's number?" Shaun jumped in.

Now he wondered why he'd brought it up. He should have kept his damn mouth shut, as he now had all their attention.

"I let you have her," Matthew said, and Rex laughed at his expense. Jess, too.

"You wish…" Luke started.

Everyone took that as their cue to leave. Rex was

first out of the warehouse, followed by Matthew. After Shaun stepped out, Jess rested his hand on Luke's shoulder, leaving just the two of them.

"Luke, just wanted to give you another heads-up on the lead you had Sienna run, the one she said was a dead end."

"She said it was red-flagged, not a dead end. The US Marshals Service used the name for a new identity for someone in witness protection," Luke said and shrugged. Something about taking Sienna's word for it didn't go over well for him, and he knew any of them on the team would've felt the same. That was the kind of oversight that could lead to one of them ending up dead. "Seems kind of odd, don't you think? You and I both know Sienna and have for a long time. Any of that sit right with you? Because it didn't with me."

Jess glanced away with a look Luke knew meant he wasn't happy about something. "Don't know," he said. "She came to me again and told me she had a word with you about this, and she just wants to make sure you understand that she was being straight about this and you need to leave it alone."

"Ah, I see," Luke said. On a mission, if he'd been told to leave it alone, that was exactly what he'd have to do. An order was an order—but not from the CIA. "So is this where you tell me to drop it, too? Because you know I can't do that. Somewhere out there is the biggest mystery yet about what happened to my dad. Maybe I shouldn't care, but I've got access to the kinds of leads that should enable me to find him."

"I said that Sienna came to me asking for you to leave it alone," Jess said. "I'm not telling you to because you and I both know this is personal for you. I'm just saying that the next time you go looking, you could raise some flags."

He just took in his boss, their team leader. For a minute, he didn't know what to say. This little warning meant he'd stepped on someone's toes, but whoever this Raymond O'Connell in Wisconsin was, he wouldn't be leaving it alone. "So what are you saying, Jess? Is this something that'll get me into hot water?"

"No, I'm saying next time, the order to leave it alone will come down from the colonel. For Sienna to come to me after this so-called favor means she wants to be sure you don't go doing any more looking into this guy. Either he's their asset or there's something else about him that has them not wanting anyone poking around. So anything you want to check out or look at, tell me, and I'll do it for you. And a word of advice: When Sienna comes asking to do you a favor again, your answer is no." Jess slapped his shoulder. "Let's get out of here. I've got things to do. Don't you have a plane to catch?"

"Yeah, and some family things, too. What about you?" he asked as he followed Jess out.

"Same old," he said. "Heading back to an empty house to take care of some personal business."

They locked up the warehouse, and he took in Jess's pickup, which was parked with Luke's bags loaded in back, ready for the plane he'd hop back to Billings, where his own pickup was waiting. Then he'd drive back to Livingston. As he settled in the passenger seat, his team leader behind the wheel, he considered everything Jess had said.

"Since you said I'm red-flagged, can you do me a favor, Jess?"

Jess pulled onto the road. "Name it."

"Find out the skinny on this Raymond O'Connell. Is it as Sienna said, or is it something else?"

Jess said nothing as he pulled onto the main road, the traffic heavy. "Consider it done. But, Luke, I have to ask you one thing about this. I know you're dead set on finding out about your dad, but you ever ask yourself whether maybe, just maybe, we might uncover something you may not want to know?"

He took in the traffic on the road ahead. "Every day," he replied, "but that's not going to solve anything now, is it? Because not knowing is worse."

Chapter 6

He'd let himself in the front door of his mom's house after parking on the road in front, because it seemed everyone was there. Owen's van was in the driveway, with Ryan's pickup beside it and Marcus and Charlotte's Subaru behind, beside Karen and her other half's Mercedes. Then there was Suzanne and her work-in-progress MGB. So much for slipping in with his case of lager, settling onto the sofa, and getting his head around his last job. His work was something he didn't talk about with his family.

He stepped inside, hearing voices from the kitchen and out back as he dropped the case of beer and his bag on the floor, then opened the closet and tucked his SIG into the gun safe on the top shelf. He kept the Glock that lived in his ankle holster where it was and closed the door.

"Hey there, you're home," Owen said, poking his head around the corner. "Didn't know you were on your way back." He looked the same as he always did, in a white shirt and faded jeans.

Luke lifted his bag and the case of beer and strode toward him, handing him the case. "Didn't know I needed to call. Put that in the fridge for me," he said.

In fact, that was something he usually did, calling his mom to give her a heads-up, but that meant, oops, she would tell every one of his siblings and they would come over, just like now.

As he strode to the end of the hall where his room was, he flicked on the lights in the bathroom and his mom's room as he passed. It was just something he did to settle in and make sure nothing could or would jump out at him.

He could hear Owen in the kitchen, talking to someone, as he settled his bag on the queen bed in his room, which seemed to never change. He opened the closet, seeing the clothes he never took with him on missions, then closed it and started back down the hall, flicking the lights back off room by room as he made his way to the kitchen.

Karen was dressed in white sweats and a loose white T-shirt, her hair the same bright red she was known for. It was shoulder length, hanging loose, unlike her usual ponytail. She was barefoot, and he took in how short she was. "Well, that was a short trip," she said. "Clean shaven, too. Where were you this time, or can't you tell me?"

He reached into the fridge for a beer and pulled one out, then twisted off the cap and leaned against the closed fridge door. He couldn't have explained it to anyone, but he needed to have something against his back as soon as he got home, stepping into this civilized life, the opposite of his other life as a team man. His family had no idea of all the things he did, the people he'd killed. The missions were all classified. No one in the civilized world had any idea of what really went on.

"You know I can't, but I do want to talk with you all about something I've found out."

What the hell was he doing? He lifted his beer and took in the way Karen and Owen exchanged a glance. He didn't miss their confusion.

"This sounds ominous," Karen said.

Owen said nothing at first as he lifted his beer and took a swallow. "And what would this something be?" He gestured to Luke.

Luke took in everyone in the backyard, who still hadn't figured out he was there. Eva was perched on Marcus's shoulders, and he was standing with Ryan, talking. The grill was unmanned. He realized this was what they always did. Even though they had their own lives, they really didn't, because they shared everything. There was Jack talking with Suzanne, and he didn't see Harold. His mom, Jenny, and Alison were at the patio table with Charlotte. It seemed everything about their lives here had continued to go on.

"There is something I want to talk to you all about —Marcus, Ryan, Suzanne, just us, no one else. So if you can set some time aside…" He could feel himself stepping into something he shouldn't, but at the same time, he didn't want to wait anymore. He could see the minute they understood this was likely serious.

"Okay, should I get them now? Because you're making me a little nervous," Karen said.

Owen leaned against the sink, saying nothing.

"You know what?" Luke said. "With everyone here, this isn't the kind of thing I want anyone to walk in on, namely the kids and Mom. How about we head out and talk somewhere else? Actually, now would be better than waiting."

He had all their attention now, and Karen's face showed the alarm he was positive she was feeling. It wasn't lost on him that Owen still hadn't said anything.

"Now you're scaring me, Luke," Karen said. "How about you spill it and just tell us? Is this work, some trouble you're in, or…"

"It's about Dad."

Karen couldn't have appeared more shocked, and Owen seemed to freeze before slowly dragging his gaze up to him. Karen reached over to touch Owen's arm as she glanced between her brothers. "You know what?" she said. "Let's meet back at my place. Owen, you bring Suzanne, and I'll tell Marcus and Ryan. If it's all the same to you, let's not wait."

He watched his sister as she stepped outside and made her way over to Ryan and Marcus, who stared at him through the window, giving everything to him. Something changed in them when they knew he was there.

The door squeaked open, and Ryan strode in, his gaze going right to Luke. Their mom was moving their way, too. Of course, she'd spotted that he was back, but right now, the last thing he wanted to do was talk about this with her.

"Didn't know you were coming in," his mom said. "Did you get something to eat?"

There was something about her, her short dark hair. Alison followed her in, and Eva too.

"Yeah, I grabbed something on the drive in," Luke said. "Sorry, I should have called."

He spotted Suzanne and Karen through the window.

Something in Suzanne's expression told him Karen had given her a hint as to what he'd said.

"But you know what? I'm actually going to head out in a minute here," he said. "There are some things I need to do."

His mom said nothing. Even Alison and Eva were watching him intently.

Just then, Karen jumped in, forcing a yawn. "Well, we're heading home. We've decided to make it an early night. It's been a long week."

To Jack's credit, he said nothing as she dragged him past. Then Suzanne made her excuses, as well. Luke lifted his beer, taking another swallow, while Marcus and Charlotte got Eva bundled up. Ryan said something to Jenny, and then it was just him in the kitchen with Owen, as his mom was seeing everyone else out.

"I'm curious, Luke," Owen said. "What is this? Dad walked out eighteen years ago, without a goodbye, so what exactly is this about? What do we need to talk about? Is this a walk down memory lane or what?"

The way his brother asked, for a minute Luke thought for sure he'd say he wasn't interested, and goodnight. He couldn't say anything in reply, as he heard the door close and spotted his mom coming their way.

"You ready?" Luke said.

Their mom walked past them and continued on into the kitchen, then lifted her hand and took them both in. "Well, what are you two waiting for? You think I don't know something's up when you show up and everyone is leaving all of a sudden? Go wherever you all are going, but if this is about a surprise for me, remember I don't like surprises."

She was a smart woman. At the same time, he

couldn't help wondering if she had any idea of what they were talking about. He didn't want to see the kind of hurt he knew the thought of his dad would bring her.

"Fine, no surprises," Luke said. "Ready, Owen?" He set his beer on the counter and tapped Owen's chest with his hand.

"I guess," Owen said.

They started to the door, and he could hear his mom moving about in the kitchen as they went out. He realized their mom seemed to have her hand in each of their lives.

Owen stopped at his van. "You want to ride with me?"

Luke took in his pickup and the houses around them, seeing suburbia, but something had the hair on the back of his neck standing up.

"Yeah," he said. "I think I will."

Chapter 7

"So what exactly is this about?" Suzanne said. "Karen said you had something you wanted to talk to us about, and it sounded serious."

Luke looked over to Karen, who was opening a bottle of white wine on the island. Ryan was perched on one of the stools beside her, and Owen had joined him, while Suzanne was on the sofa, thumbing through her phone. Marcus stood in the middle of the living room, his arms crossed, giving everything to Luke. He found himself looking for Jack, but the man was nowhere to be found. He heard Karen pour a glass of wine.

"You sure no one else wants anything?" Karen said as she lifted her glass.

Suzanne lifted her hand. "Am I going to need a drink to hear this?" She was looking at him.

He just tilted his head. "Seriously? Entirely up to you. Where's Jack?"

Karen walked around the island, barefoot again. "I told him we need to talk alone, and he said he had some things to do back at the office, so it's just us. Why don't you get to whatever you want to talk about, Luke? You said it's about Dad."

Everyone was watching him. For a second, it was so quiet in the room that he could've heard a pin drop.

"You know what I do," Luke said. "There are things I don't talk about. Well, I have access to the kind of information that isn't available to the average person."

Marcus had a seriousness about him more and more as of late, just something that came with being the local sheriff, whereas Ryan seemed not to have a clue what he was talking about.

"Something happened?" Suzanne blurted out as Karen handed her a glass of white, not something she normally drank. "Thank you," she said before giving everything back to him again. "You're making me nervous, considering every other time you come home, we find you unmoving on the sofa in Mom's living room with your head stuck in whatever godforsaken place you've been, yet now here you are." She gestured toward him with her glass.

"He said it's about Dad," Karen cut in.

He didn't know why, but he slid his gaze over to Owen, who seemed unusually tense and added nothing.

"What about Dad?" Suzanne said. He could hear the emotion and saw it the minute she sat up, stiffening. Marcus, too.

"You ever wonder what happened to him?" Luke said. "I mean, I remember it like yesterday, that morning, Mom sitting us at the kitchen table before sending us to school, saying Dad was gone and he wouldn't be back. It was just us now. I don't know about any of you, but my first reaction was not to believe it. Dad and I were supposed to go fishing that Saturday. I even went out there to our spot and waited, but he didn't show. I was convinced he would…"

"It gutted all of us, Luke," Suzanne said. "But he's gone. He took off and didn't bother with a phone call, a letter, nothing. Not even after all these years. Just showed how he felt about us."

He was a little surprised this was coming from her. Karen, too, gave her a sharp glance before dragging her gaze back over to Luke.

"I didn't know you did that," she said. "I suppose we all have our secrets about that time. I knew I was Dad's favorite. I hated Mom for a long time after. I was an absolute bitch, and you all know that. There, I'll say it. I figured she drove him away, did something that made him leave us…" She didn't finish, and no one said anything for a moment.

"It wasn't Mom's fault," Marcus said. "She's the one who stayed. He left. But what happened? I mean, does anyone know? A man just up and walks out and disappears when his kids are asleep… I know I've run checks in my system, and nothing shows up on him. Ryan, you have too. I know you told me you've had your ear to the ground."

Luke knew Ryan and Marcus had always been closer, getting in trouble together.

"Well, that's the thing," Luke said. "I've been using the resources I have available with the US military, which you should know reaches further than anything you would ever have, Marcus. I've found nothing, just dead ends. I asked myself, how is that possible? In what I do, there's always a trail, no matter how small. A man doesn't just disappear."

He knew Karen, Suzanne, and Marcus understood.

"You're saying he's dead," Marcus jumped in.

Luke just shook his head. "I'm not saying that. I can't say that for sure. In my line of work, people disappear all the time. You can be made to disappear or want to disappear. But then I found out that Dad didn't exist before 1983. Then Raymond O'Connell married Mom. As I'm looking, nothing's jiving. Then something came up in Wisconsin. It was flagged by someone I work with, who came to me, and next thing I know, I've got the CIA up my ass. My friend there did some checking and then gave me some bullshit story about how it wasn't the right O'Connell and I needed to drop it."

He took in the way everyone gave him their attention—and then there was Owen. He couldn't put his finger on it, but something was off about his brother.

"Owen, I often wondered if you knew more," Luke said. "You always had Mom's back, and even when she told us, your reaction was different. You never reacted the way any of us did. Suzanne and Karen were crying, and Marcus and Ryan were shooting off questions about where he was, but you, Owen, you always said to drop it. You said he was gone, not worth it. A piece of shit, you called him more than once."

Owen just shook his head and then gestured toward Luke. "What do you want me to say? He left. It was eighteen years ago. Why are you digging up skeletons that are best left buried? Did you ever ask yourself, with all this poking around you're doing, if it'd be better if you let it go? I mean, think of Mom. What do you think this did to her? She had to figure out how to do everything alone, and none of you made it easy on her. What's this really about, Luke?"

The way Owen said it had him pausing another second, really taking his brother in.

"This here is about answers, Owen," he said. "Don't you want to know, good or bad, what happened? Because I sure do."

"No, actually, I don't," Owen said, but then his cell phone started ringing, and he pulled it from his pocket. His expression was tense, and he pulled in a deep breath and said, "I have to go." Then he took a step, slipping his now silenced phone in his back pocket before dragging his fingers through his wavy dark hair, sweeping it back, flicking those O'Connell blue eyes toward him.

He had been there for all of them to lean on. Sometimes he hadn't been at his finest, but he'd always been there for them.

"You know what?" Owen said. "Let's just say I was once interested in knowing how a man could just up and walk out without ever calling, or writing, or stopping by. But that moment disappeared a long time ago. So my advice is to drop it. Don't look anymore. Tell yourself whatever you need to tell yourself about a man who didn't give a shit about his kids and his wife, but for God's sake, stop this. And before you all leave here, you'd better figure out a surprise for Mom, because right now she believes we're talking about a surprise for her, some gift. Come up with something, because if she knew what we were really talking about…"

Owen stopped talking and took a step toward him, then another, taking him in and not pulling his gaze. There was something there that Luke couldn't put his finger on: hurt, anger, betrayal, something. "You know when you poke into a nest of snakes, you get bit, and real bad. So stop stirring things up when they should be left where they are, buried, or someone is going to get hurt."

There it was, something in his expression as Owen stepped around him to the door and pulled it open. He stopped for a second before looking back. "I'm dead serious. Drop it, stop looking, because I remember how many nights I listened to Mom crying herself to sleep. She's happy now, and every one of you should want her to stay that way. This here…" He rested his hand on the frame of the door and shook his head as he looked out into the hall and back to them. "It's bullshit. Talking about it and stirring things up will sure as shit have something landing on Mom's doorstep. Consider that before you keep poking around. Ask yourself, if something was flagged by the CIA and they told you to drop it, maybe, Luke, should you listen?"

Then Owen was gone, the door closed.

Luke took in the shock, angst, and confusion on everyone's faces. "What the hell was that about?" he asked.

Marcus turned to him. "Don't know, but something's been off about Owen for some time."

Chapter 8

He was preparing to scramble some eggs, hearing the sound of water running in the house and knowing his mom was now up. He had slept surprisingly better, but it wasn't lost on him that his siblings were all over the place when it came to their dad.

"You're up early. You made coffee?" his mom said, running her fingers through her hair. She was wearing her blue housecoat, her hair sticking up, and she ran her fingers through it, sweeping it back. He gestured to the full coffeepot as he added oil to the pan, then put some bread in to toast. Then he reached into the cupboard and pulled out a mug to pour a cup for her.

"Thank you," she said as she took a seat on a stool at the island.

"Always up early, Mom. You know that."

She smiled as she took a sip of her steaming coffee. "You're making breakfast, too? What a treat," she added.

He really took her in, small, sweet, tough. He didn't know how she did it.

"It's not up to you to wait on me when you come home, although I appreciate it," she said. "Kind of expected you to be parked in the living room in front of the TV."

He realized there was so much he wanted to say he was sorry for, how tough he'd made it for her, all because he'd been angry as a kid, carrying a chip on his shoulder. His dad had left, and whom had he blamed but her? He wondered if that was something all kids did, considering it was human nature to assume someone was at fault.

"So you weren't gone as long this time," she said. "I take it this was an easy job?"

He poured the eggs into the pan, and when the toast popped up, he pulled it out of the toaster and rested it on a plate before setting it in front of his mom with a knife and butter. "You butter the toast," he said. "You know I don't talk about what I do, but yeah, it wasn't the same crazy shit I usually get sent to."

He reached for the spatula and scraped the eggs from the pan before tossing in some salt and pepper, then reaching for two plates from the cupboard, onto which he divided the eggs. He wondered what was going through his mom's head. She'd been there for all of them and still was, but he wondered what had happened with his dad to make him walk out. It was between her and him—but he couldn't shake the feeling that Owen might know more.

"Got something on your mind, Luke?" she said, flicking her gaze up to him.

He could see the curiosity. At the same time, he

knew she didn't have a clue what he was thinking, and he was glad for that. "Just considering some things, looking back on some things, you know, that don't feel right. Mom, do you ever think back on things and wish you could change them, make different decisions?"

She hesitated as she scooped more butter and smoothed it over the toast. "Of course," she said, "but at the same time, not really. If I went back and changed something, I wouldn't have what I have now. Where is this coming from, Luke? You out of all my kids are the least likely to go down the road of what-ifs, so what's really going on?" She set down the knife on the plate as he settled a plate of eggs in front of her, then opened the drawer, pulled out two forks, and slipped one onto her plate. "Should I be worried about something?" She frowned. Her blue eyes seemed to hold on to so much.

"No, just considering a lot of things lately," he said. "I'm entitled to, you know. Can I ask you something?"

His mom moved one of the buttered toasts onto his plate and then forked up some eggs. "Of course. What is it you want to know?"

"What did you and Dad fight about the night he left?" he said.

Her mouth was open, and instead of taking a bite of eggs, she put her fork down. He didn't think he'd ever seen this expression on her face before.

"Why would you ask that? Who says we fought?" She gestured toward him, and he didn't miss the agitation. This was just something they never talked about.

"I remember that morning when you sat us down around the table and told us. I figured you would have fought. You didn't?"

She stared at him and blinked, then opened her

mouth to say something, but she let out a breath instead. "Why would you think that?" she finally said. She was evading him. He could tell by the way she looked to the side and how uncomfortable she was.

"Now you're answering my questions with a question," he said. He took a mouthful of eggs and then set his fork down. "Come on, Mom. What's the secret? He left, so where did he go?" He knew this was something Ryan, Karen, and Suzanne had demanded to know, and Marcus too, he thought, when they were younger. His mom just shrugged.

"If I knew, I would tell you," she said. "I have no idea where he went or what happened." She played with the eggs on her plate and then put her fork down and pushed the plate away. "What is it you want to know, Luke? I realized that a man I thought I knew, after six children, was a stranger. One night, I walked into our bedroom after you kids were asleep, and he was packing a bag. I asked him what was going on, and there was nothing, no response. Then he left, walked out the door, and said he'd made a mistake. Is that what you're wanting to hear? You want to talk about this? As far as I'm concerned, your father is dead and buried…"

She stopped talking, and he just took her in. It would be so easy to tell her he'd been looking, because not talking about what happened was something he couldn't live with.

"I want to know," he said. "I think we all want to know, Mom. It's not to blame you, and I'm not angry at you, but how does a man just walk out the door and leave his wife and his six kids and never look back?"

His mom fisted her hands and then glanced over to the clock on the stove. "I have to get dressed," she said.

"I told Marcus and Charlotte I would take Eva today. She doesn't have school. Thanks for breakfast, and I'm glad your home."

She slipped off the stool, and he just watched her, knowing that if his siblings had any idea he'd brought their dad up, they'd likely be having words with him. Then his mom turned back to him and rested her hand on the countertop, smoothing it over. His cell phone rang, but he didn't answer it. Instead, he didn't pull his gaze from his mom. She likely expected he'd turn away and answer his phone, like he always did.

She pulled in one breath and then another. "You know, I have to give you credit, all of you. When your dad left, I knew it gutted you all. We were in survival mode. I picked up a job at the hardware store, and then with the city, at the waterworks, one that gave me a pension so I could retire this year. But back then, working all day and then coming home to all of you, who were angry and blamed me for your dad disappearing… Don't you think I blamed myself for so long? I wondered what I did wrong, where I screwed up. How could I not see something wrong right in front of me? All I could do was get out of bed and put one foot in front of the other, because I didn't have the luxury of wallowing in pity. I had six mouths to feed, six kids who needed me, even though each of you was furious at me. You thought I'd done something. Now here we are, and you have questions…"

She shrugged. "I don't know what to tell you, Luke. He left. If he wanted to reach out, don't you think he would have done it by now? So no, I have no idea where he went or why. Everything about your dad is a mystery to me. Anything else you want to know before I go get dressed?" Her hand was pressed to her chest, and he could feel her vulnerability and something else that he couldn't put his finger on. Evidently, there was something she wasn't sharing.

"Nope," he said. "Have fun with Eva today."

She strode away, and he listened to her door close and took in the nearly untouched breakfast he'd made for her. At least one thing was clear: He'd had questions about his dad before, but he now had that many more.

He reached for his cell phone, seeing the missed call from Jess, and there was a message, too. He dialed his mailbox and listened.

"It's Jess," he said. "You were right. I found something. Give me a call."

As Luke deleted the message and listened to his mom down the hall, he wondered what she'd say if she had any idea of what he was doing, looking for his dad. He couldn't help wondering what she would do if or when he found him.

Chapter 9

"Come on, Jess. Pick up," Luke muttered. This was the third time he'd called his team leader, and it had gone right to voicemail.

He paced the living room of the house he'd grown up in, taking in everything his mom had, everything she'd worked for. The modest furnishings were all her.

He'd waited to call Jess after his mom left to retrieve the little girl who would soon officially be part of their family. She was a mother, a grandmother, whereas the man he'd been searching for had done nothing for any of them. So, again, why was he looking?

"Hey, sorry about that," Jess said as he answered. "Got some kind of crazy-ass shit going on. I've been trying to get a hold of Matthew. You haven't heard from him, have you?"

Luke was already shaking his head as he stood at the living room window, seeing his truck parked outside. Just then, the sheriff's cruiser pulled up and parked in front of it. He took in Marcus as he stepped out from behind the wheel.

"No, I haven't," Luke said. "What's going on?"

His brother was looking at his pickup and up the street, doing the cop surveillance thing he did.

"Not sure," Jess said. "He called, left a message, said he was being followed, he thought. Someone was in his place, too. Rex said he was on his way over to Matthew's to check in, and he said someone's been asking his super about him, too, and he spotted a car following him. I've left a message for Shaun, but he hasn't called me back. When I start hearing stuff like this, I get a really bad feeling. Nothing weird at your end? People following you, calling, showing up?"

Luke just shook his head. Outside, Marcus was dressed for duty and was almost to the front door, evidently wanting a word with him. "Nope, it's all quiet. But you called and left a message, something about me being right?"

Jess let out a breath on the other end. "Yeah, the Raymond O'Connell you were checking into in Wisconsin, where Sienna told you to drop it? There's something really weird going on, because when I went in and checked, there was nothing there."

He stilled. When the front door opened, he gave everything to Marcus, who said nothing as he closed it behind him, evidently seeing that he was on the phone.

"I'm confused," Luke said. "What do you mean, nothing there?"

"Exactly what I said. It's as if he completely disappeared, no name, no address, no nothing. Raymond O'Connell no longer exists. It's as if he never did. Sienna indicated he had a file that was red-flagged for security, like with the Marshals Service or witness protection, but that's gone. I'm thinking either you found something, or you've spooked someone. Either way, he's gone, as is any record of him. You're basically back to the drawing board. All I can say is this: You've obviously stepped on some toes."

There it was, exactly what he didn't want to hear. It gave him both hope and angst at the same time. He took in Marcus, who stepped down into the living room, working a piece of gum as he crossed his arms, waiting for Luke to finish and get off the phone. He could tell he had something on his mind.

"Well, that's interesting," he said, pulling a hand over his jaw. That feeling he had, the one he got whenever someone was screwing with him or something wasn't quite right, was back.

"I guess that's one word for it," Jess said. "I'll let you know if I find something else, but in the meantime, if you hear from Shaun or Matthew, let me know. And keep an eye out there. Seems off that both Matthew and Rex have this weirdness going on. If it were just one, I'd say fine, he pissed someone off, but two from the team? Something isn't right. I'm going to call in to the colonel, as well, and Sienna."

He pulled in a breath, wondering what that was about. "Okay, you got it," he said, and then he hung up, pocketed his phone, and took in Marcus, who was standing in front of him and gestured toward him with his chin.

"Problems?" he said. His arms were still crossed, and from the expression on his face, Luke knew he had something to say to him. There was friendly, teasing Marcus and pissed-off Marcus. This one was pissed off.

"Hope not," he said. "That was Jess. I mentioned last night about how I found a Raymond O'Connell in

Wisconsin and stepped on some toes. Apparently, now it's as if he didn't exist. Gone, bye-bye. If I didn't know any better, it'd seem my looking into it scared someone. So what's up?"

Marcus was giving him everything. "Disappeared, huh? Well, maybe there's your answer and you should leave it alone. Mom's at my place with Eva. She said you asked about Dad."

Luke knew when Marcus had something on his mind, and he was sure his mom had told him more about their conversation. Marcus had likely sat her down and dragged out all Luke's questions about what had happened the night their dad left, and that was what had him beelining it over to him now.

"We've all danced around this," Luke said. "I thought it was time to ask. But Mom said she didn't know. She said he just walked out. I'm like, damn, isn't she curious? But at the same time, I could see there was more she didn't want to talk about. You want me to leave it alone, really?" He shook his head. "I can't, but if it makes you feel any better, I'm back at square one in looking for him. Starting to think the man is a spook or something, the way he can just disappear. I can't believe Mom isn't just a tad bit curious. Hell, I am. You should be."

"So what, you're going to track him down and bring him back into your life, our lives, Mom's life?" Marcus inclined his head and shook it. "No. Maybe I wondered about him. Hell, I wanted answers too, at one time, but one look at Mom's face today and I'm not interested in knowing. Do you have any idea what it would do to her?"

He said nothing as he pulled in a breath, feeling the

tension and resting his hands on his hips. His brother was challenging him. Great, all he needed was for Owen and Ryan to show up as well, because right now, he wasn't entirely sure where everyone stood in regard to good old Dad.

"I'm not planning on bringing him back here, and no, I wouldn't do that to Mom," Luke said. "I'm very well aware she was the only one here for us. She stayed while he fucked off, but at the same time, this is about having answers. I want to look him in the eye and make him tell me how he could be such an asshole. You say you were once curious, but you aren't anymore?"

"I didn't say I'm not curious. I'm saying everything has changed for me. I have a wife, a baby on the way, and Eva, whose adoption is in the works. I'm running a town here and have an election on the horizon to keep my job as sheriff. I have to make sure all the Ts are crossed and the Is are dotted. I don't have time to think about a man who's not worth it. Maybe you should ask yourself why you need to know. You have too much free time on your hands? Maybe it's time you considered finding someone, settling down."

He couldn't believe his brother had said that. "Team guys don't make the best partners or spouses, you know. I'm gone on a moment's notice. I spend more time with a team of guys than I would a woman. I'm not relation-ship material. You should know that."

He was thinking of Rosemary, though. He had her number, yet he hadn't called her. Maybe he would later that day.

Then Marcus's phone rang, and he pulled it out. "Yeah?" he started with a smile, but it quickly faded. "Whoa, whoa, Charlotte, what's going on? Slow down."

All Luke could make out was a panicked voice on the other end. His brother was staring straight at him.

"How many shooters?" Marcus said.

Luke's blood chilled, and he gave everything to his brother, but Marcus was already walking to the door.

"Get everyone there. I'm on my way. Charlotte, you stay right where you are! You do not leave that office, you hear me?" Marcus said, then pocketed his phone and turned to Luke. He already had the door open.

"Marcus, what's going on?" Luke said as he followed him.

"Not sure. Charlotte just called in a panic. Shots were fired by two different shooters at my house, where Mom is with Eva."

Luke recalled the warning from Jess about the weirdness with Matthew and Rex, even though it made absolutely no sense. "I'm coming too," he called out as he yanked open the closet door, opened the gun safe, and grabbed his SIG. He shoved it in the back of his jeans and hurried out the front door, seeing his brother already behind the wheel of the cruiser. Luke started running.

Chapter 10

The sirens cut through the peace and quiet of the neighborhood, and Luke knew they were driving into trouble. "Tell me again what Charlotte said."

Marcus was gunning the engine around the corner to his small older house, only a few blocks from their mom's. He spotted Harold up ahead, lights flashing, car door open. He was hunched down behind it, gun in hand. This was something he was familiar with. People were running, and another cop, Colby, he thought, was hurrying them along. They were total amateurs.

"Calls came in about gunfire, two guys with guns that the neighbors saw outside, one around the back of my house. Charlotte thought it was a joke until another neighbor called in, knowing we're cops and I'm the sheriff. She knew this wasn't local cops…"

Harold came on over the radio. "Hold back, Marcus," he said.

Marcus slammed the brakes and pulled up to where Harold was parked. Luke was taking in the scene, the flashing lights two doors down, where his mom's red Hyundai was parked. He was instantly hit with that awful feeling that his mom and little Eva were in danger. It was the kind of feeling he'd had only a handful of times when on a mission, knowing his team of brothers could look after themselves and get themselves out of any dicey situation. This, though, left him with a sick feeling. They were in over their heads. His mom and little Eva weren't able to protect themselves. This wasn't the kind of thing that was supposed to happen here.

He made his way behind the car where Harold was holed up, gun drawn, and Marcus joined him.

"Tell me everything," Marcus said, pulling his phone out. "Where are they? Who are they? Anyone talk to my mom?"

Luke rested his hand on his arm. "No, don't call. Something about this doesn't feel right."

Harold just shook his head. "Haven't seen them. All is quiet. Took a bullet to the front driver's side as soon as I pulled up here. Pretty sure it was a warning shot to stay back. Worse, I never saw the shooters. Still haven't. I know the first neighbor of yours to call in said she saw two men while she was watering her garden. They were dressed in black shirts. She thought they were Feds, cops or something. She thinks your mom and Eva were in the house. She ran inside when she heard a gunshot, then another. She said she was on the floor and called for help. She doesn't know if they're in the house or what."

"Not local law enforcement. A break and enter? Why the shooting?" Luke said. "Is this a mistake? What's the reason for your house to be a target, Marcus? Is someone out for blood?"

Harold was giving him everything. "Lonnie and Colby moved the neighbors out before I got here. Everyone else, I just hope they stay inside. Whoever it is hasn't taken a shot at them, but seems they don't want us coming in. No one's talked to your mom or Eva. I didn't want to call in case they're hiding. It would tip off whoever these shooters are."

"Good, okay," Marcus said. "We need to have eyes around back. I need someone to tell us who they are. The neighbors who called, where are they?"

They heard another shot. From the direction, he thought it had to have come from Marcus's yard. He peeked over the hood of the car and could see none other than Colby running the other way, now behind his cruiser. Maybe it had been another warning shot.

"Colby, you and Lonnie stay back until I figure out who they are!" Marcus said over his radio.

Luke took in the scene. Something about this seemed so much like a military attack on home soil. Was this the kind of thing his brother did every day? Something about it felt personal. "So what are we talking about, a break-in, home invasion? We need to get in there," Luke added.

"We don't know who it is or what they want," Harold said.

Marcus reached into the car for the CB radio and flicked it on, and Luke heard the bark of the loudspeaker. "This is Sheriff O'Connell," he announced. "You're surrounded. There's no escape, so come out slowly. Drop your guns—"

A bullet hit the side of the car, and Luke grabbed Marcus and kissed the ground. He hadn't seen anything except the bullet, which he didn't think had been meant to hit him, but he took in the horror on his brother's face.

"These guys aren't messing around," Luke said. "Let's take the back, find out who they are, and get in there and get Mom and Eva out."

Marcus turned to Harold. "You keep everyone back," was all he said before lifting the trunk of his cruiser and reaching in for an AR-15. He pulled on his bulletproof vest and tossed one to Luke, too.

Luke had his SIG in hand, ready, and he peeked around the car, taking a long look into the neighbor's yard. Marcus was already around the car, crouched down, and Luke moved to the house on the corner, to the back. Two houses down, behind a fence, was where they needed to go.

He took the lead, hearing his brother behind him, and stopped behind a lilac bush. He glanced once to Marcus before starting down the back way. "Stay low," he said, knowing his brother knew better than anyone that he was their best shot at getting in there.

Marcus carried the AR, and they made their way to the back of the next property, which didn't have a back fence, so he could see the small garage out back of Charlotte and Marcus's. He stopped at the corner, seeing the large yard, the swing set, and the backdoor, ajar, with a bullet having splintered the lock. He pressed his hand back to Marcus's chest as soon as he felt him move, about to race to the door to go in.

"Call it in," Luke said. "Looks like they're inside."

Marcus pulled out his cell phone, and Luke didn't know who he called. "We don't know who they are," Marcus was saying. "Looks like they fired at the back door. The deadbolt is blown off and the door is ajar."

Nothing about this was sitting right with Luke. "Have you pissed off anyone of late? Any threats against you?"

Marcus had long since spit out his gum, and his expression was tense. "More than usual? No idea. Get threats all the time, but not here, not at my home, where…" He didn't have to finish the sentence. Luke knew. This wasn't okay, not any of this.

"All right," he said. "How do you want to do this so we're not walking right into something? Seems there's a shooter out there, watching. I can't see anyone from here, but your yard, with all the bushes, you have all kinds of hiding spots. How are we going to get in without being seen?"

Marcus gestured with his chin. "We make it to the back door, and then you go around the side to my bedroom. The window is older, but you should be able to shimmy it open and climb in. The lock was busted on it. I keep meaning to fix it. Guess I will be now."

Luke just took in his brother and then the back door, the old wood stairs. They'd creak and give them away, but they couldn't wait. He shook his head, taking in the house and how quiet it seemed.

"No, we stay together," Luke said. "We'll both go in the back door. I'll go first, and you have my back. You know what I do. I'm trained in the art of hostage rescue in small, closed spaces. But you should know, when we rescue hostages, the hostage-takers aren't left alive. Just so you know, when we walk in there…"

Marcus pressed a hand to his arm, glancing at the door. "I know you're trained to kill, and you don't leave them alive so they can come back to fight you another day. You take them out. I get it, but you can't do that here, not on US soil. I need you to understand, Luke, this isn't a military mission. This is my family, my house, and…"

"Two thugs with guns inside are shooting at your cops to keep everyone away," Luke said. "You tell me how you want to play this, because I've been trained for this. When we go into something, we're prepared. We work a scenario over and over until we get it right. In close-quarters combat, you need to be prepared to shoot. I will, and I won't miss."

He knew his brother understood, as he nodded.

Luke started to the house first, keeping his head down, running fast to the back door, his gun in hand, waiting for shots to be fired. He stepped on the top step, his hand on the door, giving one glance back to his brother as he pulled it open, careful so it wouldn't creak. His gun was up, safety always off, ready to shoot. He reminded himself he was on US soil, civilization, but his mom and little Eva were inside, and the last thing he wanted was for them to be dragged into what he did, into his own hell of kill or be killed.

The door didn't squeak, and he motioned back to Marcus to keep quiet. One step in, and there was nothing. He took in the small laundry room, the small closed-off kitchen, hearing a clock tick, doing everything he could to hear or feel something.

His brother tapped his shoulder, and they stepped into the kitchen, both close to the counters. When he poked his head around the corner to the darkened living room, a gun fired. He felt the burn and heard a scream.

"The next one is in young O'Connell's head, or maybe your mother's!" someone shouted. "Drop the guns, both of you. Hands up! Stand up. Come in here."

It was chilling. Luke would have dived around the corner, but he knew he'd screwed up. He'd gone into a situation without any of the facts. This sounded personal.

"Don't hurt them!" Marcus called out. He dropped his gun, stood up, and stepped around Luke into the living room. "What do you want with me and my family? Who are you?"

There was something almost familiar about the deep voice, Luke realized. He pulled out his cell phone where he crouched in the kitchen, gun still in hand.

"Oh, it's not you I want anything with, Marcus O'Connell. Luke! Come on out, Luke! Seems we have business. I have your mother, and you have my father."

He thought for only a second before sending a quick text off to Jess: *Two shooters at Marcus's, maybe more. They have Eva and my mom. I think this is about our last mission.*

Chapter 11

"I'm right here," Luke said. "Here's my gun." He slid his SIG across the hardwood floor and stepped into the living room, seeing his mom on her knees with such fear in her face, in her blue eyes, and Eva pressed against her in her arms. A gun was held steady behind her head.

There was just one man there: brown hair, hazel eyes, thirtyish. Luke didn't have a clue who this was. He'd never seen him before. He was slender, wearing a black knit sweater, blue jeans. The gun he held was similar to Luke's, military grade.

"You seem to know who I am, but I don't know who you are," Luke said. "Tell me your name. You said I have your father, so you break into my brother's place?"

He took in the way the man stood, not nervous, comfortable with a gun, wearing gloves so as not to leave any prints. The man smiled and lifted a brow. "Stop the games, Luke. Where's my father?" he said.

He heard the deliberate click of the safety, something he did himself when he meant business, and his mom jumped.

"What the fuck?" Marcus shouted. "Get that gun off my mother and my little girl! Put it on me…" He moved forward, but Luke slapped his hand over Marcus's arm to stop him. "What the fuck, Luke? Is this about you? He knows you?" Marcus snapped.

Luke took a careful step forward, seeing everything and wondering where the other guy was—likely outside, out front, making sure no one made their way down here. That was what he would've done.

"I'm having a hard time figuring everything out," he said as he stepped in front of Marcus, not looking his way. "Who's your father?"

The man held the gun steady. It was something Luke himself had become good at from working with guns, training with them. They had become an extension of his arm, his hand. This man definitely had that skill.

"I think you know, but if you want me to say it, Stefan Schwartz. You picked him up when all he did was come forward and do the right thing, busting a company that was and is screwing innocent people. Can't believe you would defend them. considering the slope of criminality they're slipping down. Where did you take him to dump him, some military hole, a prison where they can torture him and bury him forever?"

What the hell was he supposed to say? He could feel his mom staring at him with all manner of horror. She had no idea of the depths of what he did. He heard Marcus swear beside him.

"I have no idea where your dad is," Luke said. "Tell me how many of you are here—two, three, four…?" He didn't pull his gaze from the man. "What's your name?"

"Ben, but I'm not here to get personal."

"Well, evidently, this is personal, because you're in my brother's house, and you seem to know far too much about my family. How did you find us, me?"

The man didn't smile, and Luke was very aware the gun hadn't moved, either. "Same way you found my father. You think you're the only one who has access to records? One thing my dad said was that if something happened to him, if he disappeared because he was trying to do the right thing, the men who came looking for him would be military, and they would want to make sure no one got their hands on all his classified material. You probably already know that you didn't find everything. Dad made sure of that. It's someplace very safe, where you'll never find it. I want my dad back. You know where he is."

There was something about Ben. Luke knew he was serious. There would be no hesitation. It was something in his eyes, something Luke knew all too well. When you were trained to kill, you didn't blink. You didn't hesitate.

"Okay, so you're military, too," Luke said. "My other team members, you come looking for them?"

Shit, so whatever information the CIA wanted was gone, and now his family was in the line of fire.

"Let's see. Jess, I couldn't quite nail him down. Seems he stays on base. My brothers tracked the others down. Joel was at Sergeant First Class Matthew Newman's place in Hickman, Nebraska. He broke in to leave a calling card. Liam followed Master Sergeant Rex Barnes. Then there's Shaun. Haven't been able to find him yet, sneaky bastard. But then, Martin never did do well with the whole military thing. Oh, and I think you remember my sister?"

In that second, Luke could hear his breath, long and loud, the thump of his heart. The floor beneath him was a little shaky. "Who's your sister?" he said. He wanted to swallow but didn't.

"She was waiting for you at the bar, Rosemary. Seems you had some fun. You kissed her, took her to her room. You know how we found you? She slipped from bed when you were fast asleep, and she broke into your phone and downloaded all your contacts."

Luke knew he had to be full of shit, because his cell phone was encrypted. He was shaking his head, wondering how she'd found him and how he'd suddenly become hunted.

"You know how easy it was to get into your phone?" Ben said. "Rosemary works in cybersecurity, so nothing can stop her. For a special forces man, that was sloppy on your part. So yes, Sergeant First Class Luke O'Connell, we know all about your brothers and their partners and their children, and your mother, Iris. Sorry about this, ma'am." He actually stared down at her.

Luke knew she had to be in shock, but she was handling this better than he expected.

"Seems this was the best way to get your attention," Ben said. "So now I have it, and I have your mother. If I haven't been clear enough, I want my father released. He's going to be given safe passage on a private plane to Bolivia. I want ten million dollars delivered to him, as well, so he can disappear. The evidence your country so desperately wants won't stay hidden and buried. It'll appear in every country's media room. Some will report it, expose it, and some will bury it. We'll see which independent journalists are still independent. Or the Harris Group could destroy their technology. You know what

I'm talking about. Fabricating crime scenes… Wonder if your sheriff brother here would be interested in knowing that his government and others have sold out and can now fabricate DNA and stage a crime scene? Maybe the guys you're looking for aren't who committed the crimes. Leaves you with a nice tingly feeling, doesn't it, Sheriff?"

Luke knew his brother had to be stunned. He could see him looking his way with something resembling shock.

"Luke…" Marcus started, watching with horror, way out of his element.

Luke gave everything back to Ben, who was standing there, so controlled, with his mom. "I need to make a call," he said. "I'm not in charge of the military. As you've already pointed out, I'm just a soldier, a trained one. I follow orders. There's a lot of people above me, and I have no idea where they took your father. It doesn't matter whether I agree with what they did or not. My opinion doesn't count. Where they have your dad stashed, I have no idea."

Ben slid his gaze down to his mom and then Eva, pointing the gun at one and then the other. "Then I guess," he said, "you get to choose who lives and who dies."

Chapter 12

"This isn't going to solve anything," Marcus said. "You have issues with some military operation my brother is a part of, and that has nothing do with my family, our mother, or my child. They're innocent. Just let them go. Do not make this worse for them. I told you before that you can have me. I'm the sheriff. Just think of the leverage you could gain by holding a sheriff at gunpoint. That'll have things moving much faster for you. Doors will open quickly. It'll get your issue noticed, get those in power giving you what you need to shut this down. It will get you the public outcry you're looking for. People pay attention when it's a sheriff. My mom and a little girl won't get the same attention, the same recognition."

Luke knew what his brother was doing. He could hear the panic in his voice. Not a sound had come from Eva or his mom, who was protecting that little girl with everything she had. He could tell by her face that there was no way she'd allow Ben to hurt one hair on Eva's head, the way she held her so close, her face pressed into her chest. She wasn't allowing her to look their way.

"Well, that's the thing. I can't let them go, because this is about Luke and his choice. You had a five-man team go in and take my dad, whose only crime was telling the truth and exposing a company for crimes against the public. I'm not looking for media exposure right now or holding out hope that anyone in the public would chase the CEO of the Harris Group and all the politicians in power down the street with a pitchfork. I sure as shit don't care anymore whether a public reckoning happens. We're way past that. I told my dad to let it go, that doing what he was thinking of doing would end badly and he'd get screwed, because the power these billion-dollar corporations now hold over governments has made them untouchable. He was naive to think he could bring them down. So no, request denied.

"This isn't about getting the media involved. This is about me needing a military team with the skills to get my dad out. You, Luke, are part of that team. You'll figure it out. After all, your team is part of the Delta Force, the army's best of the best. You all have the kinds of skills that mean you can get in and get my dad. After all, you guys don't really exist, do you? Every mission you do, the government can and does deny claims you were ever there. What you do tests the boundaries of legality, of human rights. Do you want to continue, or should we talk about step one and getting your team together?"

From the way Ben talked, he had a feeling he knew a lot about him and his team. This wasn't going to be a quick fix to save his family. The way Marcus was staring at him, he knew he was doing his very best to get his head around what the hell the man was saying.

"I don't care what you have to do or who you have to call," Marcus said, staring at him. "Just do it."

Luke knew the clock was ticking. *Tick tock.* "Let me make a call. But at the same time, I need you to get the gun off their heads, to let them up…"

Ben was shaking his head. "You're wasting time. Make the call now."

"I'm reaching for my phone in my back pocket," he said as he slowly reached back, keeping his other hand raised in the air. The last thing he wanted to do was spook the man. He took in the reply from Jess, several texts and two voicemails. His ringer was off.

What the hell is going on?

He pressed the call button.

"Put it on speaker so we can all hear what you're saying, so I know you're not ordering in some team to take me out," Ben said.

There was no chance of that, anyway, considering the curtains were closed.

"What the hell is going on there?" Jess said. "I still can't find Shaun, and…"

"You're on speaker, Jess," Luke said. "Just listen. I'm in my brother Marcus's house. Marcus is here listening along with my mom and little Eva. Ben, one of the sons of Stefan Schwartz, our last target, is in my brother's house and has my mother and Eva with a gun to the head. You said Matthew had a break-in, and Rex said he was being followed. You should know it's Stefan's kids, and one is looking for Shaun. Ben wants his dad released from the military prison he was taken to. He wants a private plane to Bolivia and ten million dollars.

He wants our team to get him out. You know what base they stashed him at?" He held the phone out in front of him and knew Jess needed a second, because there was silence on the line.

"Everyone has ears on this?" he finally asked.

Ben inclined his head. "Team leader Jess, you're a hard man to track down," he said. "Yes, we're all listening in, and let me be one hundred percent clear on this so there're no interruptions. Your team went in and grabbed my dad, a precise military operation. You were sent in as private security. The Harris Group board was horrified. No one knows where he is. All our calls and enquiries have turned up nothing, but at the same time, we expected it to happen. So this is how this is going to work: You're getting my dad out to keep a bullet out of the head of your teammate's mother or his little niece. The clock is ticking. I'm giving you six hours." He lifted his left hand and took in his watch. "It's nine twenty now, so you have three hours to secure his release, and in six hours he'll be on a plane to Bolivia with ten million—"

"That's impossible," Jess said. "We can't just walk into a heavily secured military base. They won't turn him over. Look, what happened to your dad didn't sit right with any of us, but let me tell you how it works in the military, in our unit, and what we signed on for."

Ben didn't laugh and didn't shake his head. "You think I don't know what your team does? Let's see. First, you don't really exist. Your recruits are all the best from the Green Berets, the Rangers, wherever you pilfer them from. You don't accept less than one hundred percent accuracy, so you really are the best of the best. Your unit is sent in for rescue operations, hijackings, to serve as bodyguards in circumstances where only the best are needed. Your training grounds are similar to a house of horrors. Every one of you is a professional soldier who hates the army. Let's not forget that you're secretly funded from government accounts, away from the public eye. How many millions do you have stashed away for that rainy day when your own government turns on you and hunts you down for the dogs you are? You know it will happen. It's just a matter of time. Let me remind you that your unit has more power and less accountability than any other military organization. So yes, you can do this. This should be an easy one for you."

Marcus was staring at him, and his mom was now also seeing him in a light he didn't want to be seen in.

"Jess, what about Shaun, Rex, Matthew?" Luke said. "Can you get them? Look, this is my family, and…"

"We'll get him," Jess said. "Ben, you listen to me. It may not be that easy for us to find where your father is."

"Really? Well, maybe you need some incentive," Ben replied, then lifted the gun and fired.

Chapter 13

He was running back to where Harold was holed up behind the sheriff's car, and he saw the moment he spotted him, the horror in his eyes. Ryan was also there now.

"What the hell, Luke? Where's Marcus? What's going on?" Ryan said, lifting his shades, on edge, alert, and shocked. "You're bleeding…"

In the distance, people were watching, everyone trying to figure out what the hell was going on. Harold was in the trunk, then pulled out a bandage and pressed it to Luke's forearm, which was dripping blood. He took the thick gauze and pressed it against the flesh wound, then took the tape Harold had ripped off and secured it in place.

"It's a scratch, is all," he said. "I've had worse."

"What's going on in the house? Mom and Eva are in there? How did you get out?" Ryan demanded as Harold radioed in for paramedics.

"Marcus refused to leave. He's staying behind with Mom and Eva. There's one guy in the house, name's

Ben, and one more out front that we know of for sure, who has good cover and a good view. If anyone approaches the house, he'll likely shoot to kill. Don't know who he is in relation to the guy inside. I'm the messenger."

After Ben had shot him, he'd yelled for him to get out, and Luke was still feeling the fear from his mom, Eva, and his brother. He could hear sirens in the background and knew this could end with his family dead. At the same time, as much as he wanted to, he couldn't share any of what he knew, because it was classified. Disclosing any of the Stefan Schwartz scenario would have him blacklisted and charged in the military. It was something that couldn't be allowed to happen, ever.

"So what the hell do they want?" Harold said to him, still holding his radio. "And who shot you?"

"It's about a classified military operation I was part of. That's all I can say. The guy shot me to make a point before telling me to go and make sure he gets what he wants."

That hadn't been the first time Luke had had a gun pointed at him, and the bullet had skimmed his arm. He knew Ben had done it to make a point with Jess, a flesh wound, with the bullet in the wall and his mom and Eva terrified. Marcus had refused to leave, and Luke feared he'd do something really stupid to get himself killed before he could fix this. His phone was ringing again, and as he spotted unmarked cars pull up, he knew the Feds had arrived.

"So what's the plan?" he said to Jess as soon as he answered the phone.

"I heard gunfire. You okay? Who's hurt?"

He was shaking his head, seeing Harold walking

toward one of the Feds, and he wondered who had called them. "Just a flesh wound. I'll heal. You called in the Feds?"

"I called in everyone," Jess said. "As soon as you texted me, I got in touch with the colonel and Sienna, too. I'm tracking down Shaun still, and I just heard from Matthew and Rex, who are on their way back here. Colonel doesn't want to play ball. Says no one is handing over Stefan."

Luke was shaking his head, furious. He stepped away to avoid the questions he could see in Ryan's expression. Of course, they didn't have a clue what the hell was going on.

"So that's it, is it?" Luke said. "You know this is my family."

"I said the colonel doesn't want to play ball, but that doesn't mean we don't. Your family is ours, and we look after our own. Rex will find out where Stefan is. We're thinking one of two spots below the airport in Richmond, Virginia. They have a secret prison underground, operated and staffed by the military, that no one is supposed to know about. You know the kind of things they do in there. That's where we're thinking Stefan is. Sienna would know, but she's not talking yet," Jess said, though Luke knew that was something he'd rectify shortly.

"You know time is not on our side," Luke said. "Find out about Stefan's family, because I'm thinking there's some military experience there. You should know, the woman I picked up at the bar in Geneva, her name is Rosemary, and apparently she's Stefan's daughter. She works in cybersecurity, hacked into my phone and downloaded my contacts, my family's numbers. So this is on me. Seems they have a tail on all of us, and I have no idea how many more are involved in the situation here. There's one shooter out front. I don't know who it is, but I'll get in there. And you should know the Feds are here now. So how are we playing this?"

Even though he stood away from Ryan, he could see his brother was trying to get a handle on the situation.

"All the Feds have been told is that this is a hostage situation. I said there's a sheriff and his family inside, and the hostage taker is wanted on multiple sexual offences, from a sex trafficking ring across state lines, and he's considered armed and dangerous." So that was how they were building the story. No one would listen to the Schwartz family. Their credibility would be gone. He could see the news trucks pulling in and knew he had to get back over there.

"Let's get down to things," Jess said. "You don't know who the shooter is, hiding out front? We need to take him out. You're alone there, so if this thing goes sideways and we don't get Stefan out, we need a plan B."

Ryan was right in front of him now.

"We've been in worse situations," Luke said. "In the meantime, see what you can find out about Stefan's family, what they do. That will give us a heads-up on what we're up against. I'm going to get the rest of my family taken care of."

Then he hung up, taking in Ryan and seeing the Feds talking with Harold, headed right his way.

"Spill it, Luke," Ryan said. "I don't care about this being classified. What's really going on?"

The Feds were moving closer.

"Look, this is what I do," Luke said. "If the guy

inside doesn't get what he wants, he's going to kill Mom and Eva. Marcus isn't going to let it happen, but there's little he can do to stop it. Right now, I need you to get Jenny, Alison, Suzanne, Karen, Jack, and Owen in one spot. Charlotte is at the station, so get them over there. Stay there. Don't let anyone in. This is personal, and let's just say that these are the kinds of people who will shoot to get what they want. They won't hesitate to hurt anyone in our family. That's all I can say."

His brother's face paled just as two Feds approached, one man, one woman, Harold with them.

"Sergeant First Class Luke O'Connell," the man said, holding up his notebook as if reading his name from it.

"Yes, and you are?" Luke said. He wondered who'd given his name, the story they were to follow. Likely the colonel or Sienna, but maybe someone else.

"Special Agents Anderson and McLeod. We understand there's a criminal inside and one hiding outside. We've been told this is a military operation, that we're to provide backup, and deadly force is to be applied."

He didn't have to look Ryan's way to see he was already in his pickup, driving away, his phone to his ear. At least he was doing what Luke couldn't for the rest of the family. Harold was staring at him in a way that told him he'd figured out there was way more going on in this situation than he was saying.

"There's one shooter hiding out front, yeah," Luke said. "He has cover, and I need to take him out, but not until my family inside are safe. So until I give the word, no one does anything." He gestured to Harold and rested his hand on his forearm. "I'm going back in, but I need you to make sure these guys don't do anything.

How are your shooting skills?" He hoped better than most.

"I hit what I aim for," Harold said.

Luke gestured to the Feds. "You stay back here and man the scene. I'm going back in, and Harold is coming with me. He'll find the guy out front, but don't do anything until you hear from me, until I get the gun away from my family and get them out of the house to safety. Until then, no one is risking their life to do anything."

<hr>

Chapter 14

<hr>

"Ben, it's Luke. I'm coming back inside. I've got the scene squared away out here. The Feds have arrived and everyone is cooling their heels," he called out as he stepped in the back door.

He didn't have to look back to know that both Harold and Agent McLeod were out there, staying out of sight. The agent had insisted on tagging along and wouldn't take no for an answer. Luke stepped into the kitchen, and the floor squeaked. His hands were up as he walked into the living room, taking in the closed curtains, very aware of the Beretta pressing into his back, tucked under his belt. Marcus was sitting and holding Eva in his lap, but his mom was still on the floor, looking tired. The expression on her face was a mix of fear and anger.

He nodded to them, then to Ben, who was sitting in a chair behind his mom.

"Well, well, what's the news, Luke? You don't mind if I call you Luke, do you? Seems formality is rather a moot point here as I get to know your family. Maybe we should talk about how well you got to know my sister?" The way he said it sounded cruel, crude.

Luke didn't want his family knowing. It was just the kind of thing one didn't talk about in polite society. "I liked your sister, but that's not why we're here. My team has located your dad, and they'll get him out. The Bolivia flight is going to be tricky—"

"Which is a task I'm sure you're up to," Ben finished for him, cutting him off, then shrugged, making a face. "Should be much easier finding a way out of this country than in a country at war, where you're hunted by the foreign armies you're fighting. You can virtually disappear here if you know how, which I know you do, so you'll get him on a plane, private, with a secret identity. Time is ticking. We're down to two hours, twenty-eight minutes, so your team had better hurry. Just so I know you're not screwing me, this is how it's going to work: You'll get my dad on the phone so I know it's him."

Luke knew this man wasn't ready to negotiate, not yet. "Seems you're the one making all the demands here. You want your father out, I get it, but you holding my family this way, we need to make some changes. My team will have him, but I'm not so inclined to get him on a plane to Bolivia to disappear while you're still here with a gun to my family. And what about your guy out front? Who is it?"

Ben rested his gun on his lap and tapped Iris's shoulder. "You have to be getting stiff," he said. "Can I get you a cushion?"

His mom hesitated, then swallowed. "Yes, that would be nice, thank you—and please let Eva go, and Marcus. You don't need them. I already told you to shoot me if you're going to, but leave her be. She's just a child. Let her and her father go."

Luke was surprised by how strong she sounded.

As his phoned dinged, Ben handed a cushion to his mom and then glanced back to him. "Well, check and see what they have. Come on, I'm sure you're dying to look at that phone." He turned to Iris, who settled the cushion under her butt on the floor. "No, I'm sorry, but the only concession I made was letting the little girl go to her father. No one's leaving. I'm so sorry."

The way he said it, Luke was convinced he'd apologize right after he pulled the trigger and put a bullet in one of them.

He stared at Jess's message: *Stefan has five children, all Americans. One's a Marine, Ben. The chick you picked up owns a cybersecurity start-up. Joel is married, a Florida cop. Liam is a farmer, and Martin is a carpenter. Their mother is dead. They were raised by Stefan. He's in Richmond, heavy security. Just hopping a plane now. Help's coming to you.*

"Well, read it off," Ben said. "Come on, I'm sure they've done some digging on my family as well, right? Let's see here. You probably already know I'm with the Marines, Sergeant Ben Schwartz, and yes, Rosemary is really good at what she does. She found you and your family."

He nodded. "Yes, you know we found that out. We found your dad. Did you want to know where he's being held? Just for the record, none of us agrees with how this went down and who's being protected. Your dad was trying to do the right thing and got screwed. They'll have your dad out, but you need to let my mom, Eva, and Marcus go. I'm here. I'm staying. You've got me, and when I say my team is on it, they're on it."

Ben stood up, gun still in hand. Luke was very aware of the locked front door. Marcus was perched on the arm of the easy chair, and he could see how tight he was holding Eva. Getting her out was first priority. Then Luke would let his brother kill him for allowing this kind of thing to touch his family.

As he stepped closer, in front of his brother, then another step, still holding his phone in his hand, his mom was too far away for him to reach. Ben was holding the gun right there.

"I see," Ben said. "So what you're looking for is for me to let everyone walk out, and then you put a bullet in me? I think not. Even though I'm a Marine and I'm good at what I do, I'm very aware you special forces guys are that much better. You're trained killers, really—but then, aren't we all?"

Luke glanced at his mom. "Ben, you ever play games with your family when you were kids?"

Ben shrugged, confusion on his face, not moving his gun. "Of course. All kids do, right? What is this? I need you to move back away from your brother."

Luke gave everything to his mom, who was giving him everything back. "Remember, Mom, all the games you played with us as kids, you and me, like duck, duck, goose?"

He took in the expression on his mom's face. She seemed to get what he was saying.

"What is this about kids' games? I asked you to move," Ben said.

Luke stayed where he was. There was another ding on his phone: *On three.*

He let his phone drop to the floor, grabbing his gun from behind him. "Duck!" he yelled, and his mom moved fast, down on the floor, as he fired one bullet dead center in Ben's head.

Just then, the front door crashed open, and he watched as the man who'd threatened his family dropped to the ground, dead.

Chapter 15

Things weren't supposed to happen this way in his small hometown.

This was his home, a place so removed from his world, untouched and safe, that he came back there to try to forget the horrors of the outside. Now he couldn't shake the fact that he had brought the horrors of what he did, the bad, the deceitful, the horrible, right to the doorstep of his family, who had never signed up for this.

A large dark hand gripped his shoulder. "You okay?" said Shaun, who was dressed in faded blue jeans and a white and black T-shirt, his pistol holstered by his side. He was carrying his long-range sniper rifle and wearing his ballcap turned backwards. He had about an inch on Luke.

"I don't know," he said. "Ask me next week after this sinks in."

He took in the scene, standing outside his brother's house by the lilac bush he knew Charlotte loved, next to the body of the second man, whom they'd just ID-ed.

He was all in black, dark haired with a beard, a friend and fellow Marine of Ben's, with a bullet in his head courtesy of Shaun.

There were flashing lights everywhere, and he needed another minute as the adrenaline pumped inside him. His hands were shaking, his legs. He was very aware of how badly this could have gone for his family, for him.

"So how did you know?" he said. "Jess couldn't get a hold of you."

He still couldn't believe Shaun had come through the door after sending him that last text. It was something he and his team did, knowing each other's moves and thoughts because of how hard they had trained, side by side, over and over, so much so that they were synchronized and had each other's backs.

"Just had a feeling, you know, from the minute this op went down," Shaun said. "There was something off about it. Then, getting home, I never shook that feeling that had me looking over my shoulder at every street corner. Then I saw someone following me. After I led him on an obstacle course and he lost me, I followed him and cornered him on a dead-end road, knocked him out, dumped him in my trunk, and took him home to my garage. It was Martin Schwartz, a carpenter who didn't even know how to hold a gun, scared shitless. He told me everything. I didn't have to push that hard. I had a day's notice and drove all night. Saw Jess's message, but as I drove, I knew the element of surprise was on my side if no one knew where I was, so I went dark."

Something about Shaun seemed so steady. He knew his comrade didn't miss how shaken he was, especially considering Luke never got rattled. There was something about the adrenaline from this kill, especially when his family had been in the line of fire, that had him on edge in a way he'd never been.

"They'll be fine," Shaun said, resting a hand on Luke's shoulder again. "Just give them some time. They're alive."

Luke took in the Feds and a team of spooks, as well, cleaning up the scene. An ambulance that wasn't local and two paramedics he'd never seen before wheeled in a gurney with a body bag to clean up the mess in the front yard, and he watched as they took out the body bag carrying Ben Schwartz. The media circus was being held back, but the cameras would be flashing. His mom was sitting in the back of an ambulance, and Marcus was there too, holding Eva. Luke didn't think he would let her go.

Shaun's phone rang, and he answered and stepped away. Luke was still having a hard time figuring out what to say as Harold strode over to him, leaving Agent McLeod to walk back out the front gate to his partner.

Harold ran his hand over his face as he took in the body and then Luke. "This is quite the shitshow," he said. "You should go talk to your mom, to Marcus, check in with your family. Dare I ask who all these agency people are? CIA, FBI, and what other obscure agencies are they from?"

They both stepped away as the two paramedics moved in and picked up the body, then zipped him in the body bag. He turned away with Harold, taking in Shaun. Whomever he was talking to, he didn't have a clue.

"How about you don't ask, since I can't say?" Luke said.

"So what kind of spin are they going to give this in the media?" Harold said. He was a smart man, so of course he knew the truth would never get out.

"Not sure, but it will be downplayed. A gas leak or a burglary gone wrong or something."

Harold just nodded and ran his hand over his face again. He was a strong, solid cop, and Luke was glad his brother had him. He was good for his sister, too.

"You should check on Suzanne and the rest of the family," Luke said.

Harold just nodded and then gestured with his chin over to where Marcus was talking to his mom, a paramedic, and one of the Feds, he thought. "You should, as well. Finish up here and go talk to your family. Have you thought of what you're going to tell them? I don't know how to explain this."

Yeah, he'd be peppered with questions. Karen and Suzanne wouldn't buy any of the front-page story that would come out. "I'll figure something out," he said, then rested his hand on Harold's shoulder. Shaun had started back to him. "Give me a minute here."

Harold must have understood, as he didn't say anything else, just started walking, following the two agency guys posing as paramedics as they wheeled the body to a second ambulance. He nodded to Shaun and made his way out into the street where Marcus was.

Luke needed to get over there, but it was killing him inside to think of what that little girl had just endured yet again. Then there was his mom, whom he'd been giving the third degree just that morning.

"That was Jess," Shaun said, looking around as if

waiting for something or someone else to spring out from around the corner. It was just something they did. "Stefan is now in the wind."

Luke wasn't sure he'd heard him right. "What do you mean, in the wind?"

"You need me to spell it out? He's on a small private plane to Bolivia. Rex, Matthew, and Jess secured Stefan, but at the same time, we can't stand for anyone putting the gun to the heads of our families, your family. You know that. The siblings, Liam and Joel, they're tracking each of them down. They'll either walk away or have the same fate as Ben. Martin—who is still tied up in my garage, by the way—said Ben was the one who outlined the plan and masterminded this whole 'Free Daddy' thing. He organized them, but it was always about their dad. As for the woman, Rosemary, that one's your call. As far as Jess said, she did her part and passed along the information from your phone."

He pulled in another breath, considering, as he took in his family. "She's in the wind?" he finally said. He shouldn't have cared, but there was something about all of it that didn't sit right. She'd betrayed him, just as he'd betrayed her father.

"Nope, right where she's supposed to be," Shaun said. Then he slapped his shoulder and stepped away. "You let me know if you want some help there."

Luke just nodded, knowing he needed to figure out what to say to his family. "Thanks, but right now, she's way down on my list of priorities," he said. Then he started across the small front yard of his brother's house, not knowing how they'd be able to spend a night there. The cleanup would happen inside, but the memories would linger.

He dug into each step, taking in his mom, who had a paramedic taking her blood pressure, and Marcus, who was holding Eva. She hadn't lifted her head from Marcus's shoulder.

"Hey, how's she doing?" Luke said. He stopped in front of Marcus just as Harold started walking away, over to his cruiser, parked along with the media circus.

"Scared, shaken…" Marcus started, and Luke didn't know what to say to him, feeling ashamed and responsible for this entire nightmare.

"I'm sorry this happened," he started.

Marcus didn't nod, and for a second, Luke felt the anger his brother was entirely justified in feeling toward him. "You know what? Let's not do this right now. I need to get Eva settled, and Mom, too. I'll take them back to the house. We'll talk later."

The way his brother said it, Luke knew Marcus needed a minute to get past what had happened. He could feel the rift between them and the blame he couldn't fault him for. He stepped away and over to his mom, who was spattered in the blood of the man who'd held a gun to her head. He took in her spooked eyes. Shock, fear, completely shaken.

He stopped in front of her and gestured to the paramedic he recognized, who used to work with Suzanne. He must have understood, as he stepped away, giving them some space.

"Are you okay?" It was the only thing he could think to ask. "I am so sorry, Mom, for all of this. I took quite the gamble in assuming you'd remember that game you and I used to play…"

She reached out and grabbed his forearm, her grip strong. The blanket around her slipped off her shoulders. "How could I forget? You boys would insist on dragging me into the dirt on the ground, drop and run. And none of this is your fault, Luke. You saved us. If it hadn't been for you and Marcus showing up, I don't want to think of what would've happened…"

He could hear the emotion in his mom's voice that he knew she was doing her best to hold on to. Then she cleared her throat, and when she lifted her gaze to him, her blue eyes weren't filled with the same teasing that was often there with her kids.

"Mom, you're being rather kind, considering this shitshow was because of me and something that happened…"

His mom held up her hand and shushed him, and he stopped. "This was a bad day, Luke, no doubt about it. I'd like to say I've had worse, or close to it, but… You think I don't know what you do? Of course I have an idea. Of course I knew what you did, even without knowing the details of it. Some pretty bad things go on in this world that we've been sheltered from because we live here, and I'm thankful for that. I don't know how you do what you do, Luke, but every time you came home from your war, I could see it took you a while to get your footing. Now I see why. I'm not angry at all. I know you have questions about your dad, what happened, why he left. Maybe I didn't tell you everything I knew, but…"

He reached over and touched his mom's arm. "You know what, Mom? Seems it's rather a moot point right now. I'm sorry I pushed."

Marcus was striding their way, still holding Eva.

His mom nodded. "I understand why. We're a family, but sometimes it's best to leave things where they are and not dig up skeletons, not ask questions no one wants the real answers to. As you know, not everything is so black and white…"

"Mom, you need to go to the hospital and get checked out," Marcus said. "I'll meet you there with Eva."

Eva looked up at Iris, who reached out and ran her hand over her back.

"Hey there, little girl," she said. "You and Grandma are going to be fine."

"Grandma, he tried to hurt you and me. I don't want to go back there."

Luke could hear in her voice how scared she was, and he wished he could do something for her.

"We're going to stay at Grandma's for a little bit," Marcus said. "So don't think about that."

As his mom stood up, he took in how shaky she was, and he rested his hand on her arm and helped her into the back of the ambulance, though all the while she said, "You know I'm fine."

"I know, Mom, but just humor us. As you said, this is what I do, and it's not the kind of thing I ever want you to see again."

Marcus still appeared as if he had something on his mind, as if he wanted to have a talk with Luke. Iris must have understood, as she sat on the bench in the ambulance and let him step back as the paramedic closed the door. He stood with his brother for a second, taking in the scene that had already been almost entirely cleaned up.

"See you at Mom's," Marcus said.

Luke was still watching the tiny house where his brother lived. "Yeah, and then I guess I'll have to figure out how to explain this to everyone," he replied. He wasn't sure what his brother was going to say.

Marcus simply turned and gestured as he started walking over to where his cruiser was parked. "You will, at that—but at the same time, keep in mind that the whole story may not be what everyone needs to hear."

Chapter 16

Shaun had left as quietly as he'd shown up, and Luke had talked to Jess an hour earlier. They'd really busted Stefan out, and their secret black fund stash was now short ten million dollars in exchange for the missing documents no one wanted to come to light. Stefan had apparently taken the money happily, and his son Joel had turned over the documents. Stefan was now on an old Cessna to Bolivia. Meanwhile, the colonel was running a different narrative, as the missing documents the CIA wanted were now the only leverage the team had.

His mom was okay, being fussed over in the kitchen, surrounded by Jenny, Alison, Suzanne, and Karen. Charlotte was there too, and she hadn't let go of Eva for a moment.

Luke settled in the living room corner with his back to the wall, staring at the door, as Ryan rested a beer on the sofa table in front of him. The game was on TV and the sound was low. Marcus was lounging in the chair across from them, Harold was sitting on the end of the sofa, drinking a beer, and Owen wandered in behind Ryan, holding a glass of what looked like whiskey. Jack, Karen's husband, whom Luke didn't have to explain any of this to, was also holding a tumbler of whiskey.

Everyone was rattled, and he hadn't figure out what to say to them. They were still getting their heads around what had happened. Crime scene tape surrounded Marcus's house, and the news channels had sensationalized the entire story.

"They're reporting that two former Marines who had been given a dishonorable discharge were tied to a string of robberies and assaults going door to door across state lines," Owen said. "So how much of that is true?"

"None of it, or all of it," Jack jumped in. "Wasn't sure the spin it would be given, but I expected something a little more creative than downplaying it."

Luke lifted his beer and took a swallow, then played with the label on the bottle. "Eva's pretty shaken. How's she doing, and Charlotte?"

"Shaken up," Marcus said. "Eva's scared to go back in the house, so Mom is insisting we stay here, which we will until we find another place to move to. This is just added stress Charlotte doesn't need right now."

Something about sitting there made Luke feel as if he were waiting for everyone to pepper him with questions. "You all know that isn't what happened," Luke said. "They were two active military men, but that's not how it played out. We need to talk about what happened? Mom never heard them come into the house. He had a silencer on the gun that took out the lock on the back door. She was in the bedroom with Eva when she saw him and screamed, and he had her on the floor in the living room because he knew we'd come. She sat there with a terrified Eva for nearly an hour, her phone ringing and her not being able to answer. She'd have taken a bullet for her." Luke gestured toward their mother with his chin. He could see how this wasn't sitting too well with his brothers. "Suzanne is going to want to know the skinny, and so is Karen."

Marcus lifted his beer and took a swallow. "I think we all do, but at the same time, we know you do things you can't talk about."

"What can you tell us, Luke?" Ryan asked from where he stood now, looking down at him.

"All I can say is that it seems more and more as of late that my team has become like corporate security. I think if the American public really knew the things we did, they would be horrified, and it's not sitting right with me. Seems the game has been changing. It feels as if I've become a hired thug on the payroll of our government, and this time it brought the war to my doorstep." It was so quiet in the living room that he could hear the voices of the women in the kitchen. "I always feared that something could come back on us one day, and this time it did. I guess I have to ask myself if a time will come that I'll consider throwing in the towel and saying goodbye."

"You thinking of retiring from the army?" Marcus asked.

"The day will come, but not yet," he added. "I didn't really answer your questions, but not sure what I can say freely."

Marcus pulled in a breath and lifted his beer. He'd heard almost everything, having been in that living room with Ben. "You've said enough, and you know what? It's over. Some things are best left unsaid."

Luke took in Owen and Ryan, who were watching Marcus carefully. He knew what his brother wasn't saying, which was that Luke also needed to let go of the questions surrounding their dad.

"Guess you're right, big brother," he said, and as he looked around at his brothers, and Jack and Harold, he realized that the questions were completely irrelevant, anyway, because the only thing that was important was his family.

Chapter 17

L uke heard the water running, then footsteps in the hallway, and he looked over to see Marcus yawning, wearing blue jeans and an open shirt, evidently just out of bed. It was early, just past dawn, and although Luke had slept well, considering, he had heard his brother up a few times the night before.

"Do I need to ask how everyone is?" he said.

Marcus simply lifted a brow and gestured to the coffee Luke had made a little earlier. Luke took that as his cue and pulled a mug from the cupboard, then poured Marcus a coffee and rested it on the island.

"Guess you're not going to add cream and sugar?" Marcus said, and Luke took him in as he reached into the fridge and pulled out a carton of cream, then smelled it before dumping it in his coffee.

"I'm not your wife," Luke said. "Speaking of which, how's she doing?" He slid the canister of sugar over along with a spoon. He knew that Charlotte being pregnant put Marcus more on edge.

"Sleeping," Marcus said. "Eva was up a few times,

nightmares. She's sleeping with Charlotte now." He ran his hand over the back of his neck while stirring in his sugar, then lifted the mug and took a swallow. "Sorry to kick you out of your room, but thanks for that."

What was Luke supposed to say? "It's the least I can do. I'm fine on the pullout downstairs."

Aside from the two single beds in the upstairs bedroom, where Eva had been sleeping, his bedroom was the only other spare room with a big enough bed for Marcus and Charlotte. His mom had long since gotten rid of the rest of the beds in the home.

"I sleep in a lot of places less comfortable, so no big deal for me," he continued. "You know, Marcus, if you want to put your fist in my face, I understand. I'd even let you."

Marcus made a face as he took another swallow of coffee, then set his blue eyes on Luke before shaking his head. "No, I think not. It wouldn't solve anything."

"No, but maybe it would have you feeling better, at least." He poured himself another coffee.

Marcus seemed to be considering something. "You know what, Luke? I guess I just don't understand what happened. Reasonably, it's not your fault, but I can't shake it. That job you did, the one you were asked to do, it'll have me wondering now whenever I go into a crime scene. It's changed everything, knowing that innocent people who've stepped on the wrong toes are going to find themselves locked up. I know Charlotte is scared because of what almost happened, and the fear in Eva… Her living with a cop should make her safer, not put her in the line of fire. I'll have to tell Reine what happened. Could it jeopardize the adoption? Absolutely."

He didn't know what to say to fix this for his brother.

"Luke, I know you feel responsible, but you're not. As I told Charlotte, it could just as easily have been me targeted for being sheriff here. I've made a lot of enemies and could end up with some angry family coming after me, targeting Eva and Charlotte. Maybe this was the wakeup call I needed."

He could see how tired his brother was. "So what the hell does that mean, putting your family in a glass bubble? You can't do that. You can't live that way. Honestly, I never would've imagined that this could come and land on our doorstep, putting all of you in the line of fire. Honestly, I don't know what I could have done differently."

Even as he said that, though, he thought of Rosemary, the woman he'd slept with in Geneva who had somehow managed to download all his contacts from his phone. She was someone else he needed to settle things with.

"I guess I haven't asked because I know there's so much you can't talk about," Marcus said, "but tell me this: Have you fixed things there so nothing else can come back on Charlotte or Eva again? Then there's Mom and everyone else—and that includes you too, Luke. This is home, and we shouldn't ever have to worry about some military operation landing here in our hometown."

What could he say? Before this happened, he'd never have considered something like this following him home. It would've been inconceivable. He was still having trouble getting his head around it.

"We settled things, fixed things," he said, "but there's one person I still need to set right. I hope you're not going to ask for details, because I won't tell you."

An odd smile touched his brother's lips as he shook his head and put his coffee down. He lifted his hands. "I've learned long ago not to ask, and honestly, I don't want to know. I need to get showered. I told Charlotte to sleep in and not come in until later. First trimester, you know. She's really tired to begin with, and I promised her I'd find us a new place to live. There's a new house across the street from Ryan and Jenny that I'm looking at. I'm also looking at a security system for Mom's house."

It was something Luke should've been all over. "I'll take care of the security system," he said. "You just look after your family."

Marcus lifted his coffee again, then stopped. "Oh, I thought you should know: City council has been all over this. A call came in from the DA about the word from the Feds, you know, that bullshit news story. Officially, I'm not allowed to talk about what happened, and nor is anyone in the department, because it's a matter of national security. If we do, federal charges will be filed against us…" His brother stopped talking. Luke could see this wasn't sitting right with him. "As for the neighbors, they've been paid a visit by some Feds, as well, to advise them of the ongoing investigation. They're not allowed to talk about it. They were given the same bullshit line, you know, to scare the shit out of them. If they talk, they could be in a heap of trouble. So, in other words, we've been effectively handled. How often does this kind of thing happen? You know how it makes me feel to be told I can't talk about the truth?"

What was he supposed to say to that? Sometimes

Luke didn't let it get to him. He'd always been able to shut it out, but there were those missions, those targets, that left him with too many sleepless nights.

Marcus took another swallow of coffee and then jutted his chin toward Luke's arm, which was still bandaged from the bullet that had grazed him. "How's your arm?"

He'd had worse, he thought. Of course he had. "Fine, just like I told everyone. It was just a flesh wound. It'll heal."

His brother just shook his head. "You should've had it stitched up, tough guy."

Instead of saying anything more, because he likely knew it was falling on deaf ears, Marcus strode down the hall and into the bathroom.

Luke listened to the shower come on as he took in the white gauze bandage, then pulled it off. The scab was thick and deep. It would be just another scar with just another story behind it.

Chapter 18

As he sat in his pickup truck, Luke thumbed through his phone and his contacts, staring at her name, Rosemary Brooks, from Indiana, and her number. He was parked at the end of his brother's street, where the yellow crime scene tape was now gone.

What was he supposed to do with her? Jess had left the decision up to him, but then there was Marcus, who expected him to take care of every loose end of this shit-show so no part of it could ever touch his family again, and that would include Rosemary.

He considered what to say, what to do, as he stared at the phone number of a woman he wasn't sure how he felt about. When he met her, her name, what she did, and why she'd been there in his hotel bar had been shrouded in deception. He was still having a hard time getting his head around the fact that she'd been the hunter, and he and his team had become the hunted. It was a sick twist, something he wasn't used to.

He still had a whole bunch of questions he needed

answered. Remembering his fond feelings for someone who had been trying to hurt his family spurred his anger and his need to settle the score.

Then there was his dad, who seemed so much on the back burner now. Whether he'd ever have answers about him, he wasn't sure it mattered now. He was still trying to process the danger he had put his family in. As Marcus had said, he needed to let it go—and maybe he did, considering the stress his family had been under.

He held his cell phone to his ear, listening to the ring, half expecting it to be a wrong number, then heard a click.

"Hello?"

He was positive it was her voice. "Rosemary, this is Luke."

There was silence for a second, but he could hear her breathing. "I guess I should've expected you to call."

That was all she said. He found himself looking up the street of older family homes, suburbia, a place that never should've seen an enemy attack. His brother's house was just a rental, and he knew he was having to deal with too many questions from the landlord. He'd be on the hook for rent, damages, and whatever else the landowner deemed necessary, but Marcus had been the first to decide he couldn't have Eva or Charlotte living back in that house. The memories alone were too much for little Eva, and then there was Charlotte, whom Marcus had become all protective of, considering she was pregnant.

"I wasn't planning on calling," Luke said. "So was any of it true in the bar, in the hotel? And why me?"

Maybe that was what bothered him most of all, the

fact that she'd picked him. Or had she, considering he was the one who'd walked over to her?

"I think you're confused on one thing," she said. "You're the one who came on to me, walked across the bar to me, and bought me a drink. Or is it that you think I somehow made you do that? That would be an amazing trick if it were true."

Her voice was pissed off, and he found himself shaking his head as he took in the car pulling up in front of his brother's house. The trunk was lifted, and a for-sale sign came out. A realtor. Evidently, that was one way for the landlord to handle it.

"Okay, point taken," Luke said, "but then there's the story you offered, and the French accent—which left after a few drinks. Guess it was too hard to keep up the act. I'm surprised you gave me your phone number, considering everything else was false."

"What was false?" she snapped. He could hear something in her voice as if she'd been crying, some-thing she couldn't hide.

"Well, your name, for one. You said your name was Rosemary Brooks. Then there's what you do for a living. Online advertising is what you said, but we know that's not true. Cybersecurity? You're good. Never saw that coming."

"Brooks is my last name," she said. "It was my ex's. I'm divorced. And online advertising isn't that much of a stretch. But you, Luke, what did you tell me about yourself? There was no truth on your end. I was the one at the end of the bar. I didn't target you. You walked down to me. You're a military operator, so who was playing whom? It wasn't just me. At the same time, I guess I need to say thank you for my dad. You got him out."

"We always do. That was what we agreed to."

"You didn't have to kill him—Ben."

He wiped his hand over his face, shaking his head. "Consider that a mercy," he said. "He went after my family. You don't put a gun to my mother and my six-year-old niece. He crossed a line. Death was too good for him." He needed to end this, to get off the phone, but he still wanted to know how she could target innocent people, his family.

"Ben always was a hothead," Rosemary said. "But, Luke, my dad never should've been arrested. He never should've been sent away like he was. He was just trying to do the right thing. I can't believe you wouldn't be horrified about what he uncovered and tried to expose. We were left with no choice. Your government would never have let him go. He wouldn't even have been given a trial or a lawyer. He'd still be sitting in some hole, buried for the rest of his life…"

"They're your government too, Rosemary—and I don't get to pick and choose what I agree with in the military. I follow orders. Besides, this is all kind of a moot point. I don't even know why I called. Maybe curiosity. Us having drinks and you taking me up to your room, was that your plan? Would you have slept with anyone else on my team? How did you know we'd even be in the bar? It seems you were waiting. I just don't get it. Let's start there, because you have a lot to answer for."

She sighed. "You know what? That's a lot of questions, and I'm not sure I want to answer you. How do I know you're not going to come after the rest of my family—Joel, Martin, Liam? By the way, they're scared shitless right now. Would you kill them too, and me, for our hand in getting our dad out?"

Outside, the realtor was now hammering the sign into the ground.

"What part did you have in threatening my family?" Luke said. "Did you know Ben held a gun to the head of my mother and my little niece? Do you know the nightmares she has now? You think that's fair, doing that to a little girl? So why me? Why my family? You didn't answer me. Would you have taken anyone on my team to your room?"

Why did he want to know so bad?

"Honestly, I never planned to take you to my room," she said. "There was something about you that had me acting against my better judgement. I'm sorry, Luke. I would never have been part of something that put your family in danger like that, or a little girl. We didn't know Ben would do that. However, I think saying I'm sorry for something I didn't do would be the same as you saying you're sorry for taking my dad, don't you think?" She sighed again. "Your family was innocent, and so was my dad. I don't think there's anything else to say, is there?"

"Actually, there's a lot to say, a lot of answers I need. How did you even know where we were?" He realized he could go on and on, but there was something different about talking on the phone and not looking someone in the eye. He couldn't tell when she was lying to him.

"I don't have answers to give you," she said. "I think it would be best if I said goodbye. You killed my brother for what he did. Was there another way? Of course there was. So I think we've said all we need to. Goodbye, Luke."

Then she hung up, and he pulled his cell phone away from his ear. As the realtor drove off, he took in the house and thought of his brother, Charlotte, and Eva, who were now staying at his mom's. He'd go back home and see them.

Talking to Rosemary had accomplished only one thing: It had left him with the need for more answers. He needed to make sure with one hundred percent certainty that nothing about her could come back on him and his family.

Maybe he wasn't all that trusting, but what had kept him alive so far was expecting the unexpected.

Chapter 19

Luke strode down the hall of the base, his boots squeaking on the hard floor, which always appeared freshly washed. He didn't know why, but he found himself looking over his shoulder and wondering if Sienna was around, because really, he needed to address his issues with her even though finding his dad and getting answers about him were now way down on the list of his priorities. After everything, his questions about his dad didn't seem important anymore.

As he thought about Rosemary and Sienna, he was starting to wonder who was more deceitful. Sienna had backstabbed him by going to Jess like she had. What was she really up to? Was she behind the disappearance of the Raymond O'Connell he had found in Wisconsin, creating an entire cover story about witness protection, or had that identity vanished all because he was asking? A coincidence, really. But Luke didn't believe in coincidence.

It seemed his need to find his dad had shifted to a

need to deal with two women. Sienna was blowing him off by sending him toward dead ends, and it had him trusting her less than he had before. Asking the wrong questions could have him or any member of his team dead. Would she willingly toss them away or lead him and his team as sacrificial lambs to the slaughter? At one time, he'd have said no, but now he couldn't. What he'd discovered kind of blurred the lines of who was and wasn't a criminal.

As had been pointed out to him, no missing person report had been filed about his dad, because he'd simply walked away, and his mom had never questioned it. He couldn't get her words out of his head. How could a man simply disappear as if he'd never existed? Was his dad a spook or something? Maybe, but then, he could be seeing ghosts because of what he did and because of the game Sienna seemed to be playing.

He took in the halls of the base, seeing the secure room ahead with its door closed. He dropped his cell phone into the plastic slot attached to the wall, which held the phones of everyone who walked through that door. Classified was classified, and certain procedures still had to be followed.

He punched in the code and strode through, seeing Jess, Rex, Matthew, and Shaun already there, and the colonel too. Something about Jess's expression would have been unreadable to anyone else, but Luke knew something was up.

"Well, glad you're here," the colonel said. "Seems that little incident in your hometown has landed an entire shitstorm of problems on my desk. I was just asking everyone here if they had any idea how the target, Stefan Schwartz, could suddenly disappear from a secure facility, but it seems you're all suddenly playing deaf and dumb." The way he barked it out sounded accusatory.

"Colonel, are you in some way trying to hold me responsible for what happened to my family, my mother and little niece? You know why harm came down on them. It was because of something we did while doing your dirty work, the dirty business of this government." He knew he was out of line, but he didn't give a shit and could feel his adrenaline pumping as he fisted his hands. Out of the corner of his eye, he could see Jess perched on the end of the boardroom table, just shaking his head, pissed, angry, feeling exactly what he was feeling.

"You challenging my authority there, son?" The colonel stepped around the table and up to him as if he could kick his ass even though he was several inches shorter than Luke. He knew he was daring him to hit him, to do something so he could toss him in the brig.

"Oh, I'm sure you'd love that, wouldn't you, Colonel?" Luke said.

Then Matthew was there, his hand on his shoulder in front of him, pushing him. "Walk away," he said, moving him back.

"Colonel, you are way off base here," Jess said. "My team is owed an apology. I already told you we have no idea about Stefan Schwartz. He's in the wind? We did our job, turned him over. Take it up with whoever was holding him."

Luke could no longer see the colonel because Matthew was in his face, holding him back. Maybe he'd thank him later, but right now he wouldn't have minded putting a fist in his face.

"You'd better hope you weren't involved, Sergeant

Major, for your team's sake, because if you were, there'd be nothing I could do to save you," the colonel said, then walked out of the secure room. The man wanted heads to roll.

For a minute, no one said anything.

"You take care of your problem?" Jess said.

Luke knew he was referring to Rosemary, and he hesitated. "Working on it. I'll be taking care of that next. But something about this has bothered me and doesn't quite sit right. How did she know we were there? Don't any of you wonder about how convenient that was? That kind of information about our team isn't just out there, you know."

Shaun, whom Luke still owed a world of thanks, was leaning against the back wall. Next to him was Rex, whose expression told Luke he'd just figured out what he was getting at.

Rex glanced over to Jess and then Shaun. "Yeah, that's kind of creeping me out a bit."

Jess said nothing, just taking him in.

"You know what?" Luke continued. "I have a bunch of questions about all this. One of them is about Sienna. Matthew, you were pretty cozy with her at the bar. I think we need to have a talk about her, because I'm starting to wonder if she was behind what happened. One of Schwartz's sons turned over his documents, but we didn't get them all. Sienna certainly didn't get them for us. The rest were missing, remember? Maybe she had something to do with my family suddenly coming into the line of fire."

Jess was shaking his head.

Matthew was right in his face now. "You'd better

watch yourself, Luke. I was friendly with Sienna, but if you're saying I'm part of this in any way…"

Jess was already there, pulling him back. "Knock it off," he said. "Luke isn't saying that, but what was that with Sienna, anyway?"

Matthew didn't look too happy to be questioned. "Flirting. Who gives a shit? She's attractive. We were done our job and blowing off some steam. She's single, I'm single. Why does it matter?"

The way Shaun was watching them, Luke wondered what he was thinking.

"You really think Sienna was behind that when we already know the woman you picked up in the bar got into your phone?" Rex added.

Luke didn't know what to say. "Well, think about it. How did she get there? How did she know it was us? It was quite a coincidence, all of it. I think Sienna knows more."

Jess gave him everything, hard, intense, then pulled in a breath. "Well, let's find out for sure. Luke, you need to go take care of that business with the girl. Matthew, since you're more friendly with Sienna, go and work our CIA agent and find out what it is she's done, what she knows, and whether she had a hand in any of this. If she did, I want to know exactly how."

Chapter 20

Of all the places he'd never been, Terre Haute, Indiana, was one of them.

As he pulled up in his rental car and parked in front of a two-story home with a porch and a black Jeep in the driveway, the street reminded him of his hometown in some ways. He took in the neighborhood, seeing kids on bikes, and started up the sidewalk. The oak tree out front had to have been one of the reasons she owned this place. It was the perfect climbing tree and gave the area an established feel.

He strode up the three steps and tapped on the screen door, which was open. He could hear her voice inside. The sun was out, and he was already sweating. She came around the corner and stopped with the phone to her ear. She was barefoot in a gray sundress, and her hair was pulled up.

"Larry, I'm going to have to call you back," she said. Then she hung up the phone and stood there for a second, just staring at him. What was it about her? Time seemed to stand still. "What are you doing here?" she said, but she didn't take a step closer to open the door to him.

"We have some things to discuss," he said. "Open the door."

She hesitated, then set her phone down on the hall table before flicking a small metal latch and pushing the screen door open with a squeak. "I guess I should thank you for not breaking the latch on the door," she said.

He stepped inside, taking her in, remembering how good her body looked naked. He had to remind himself his family had been in danger because of her. "I'm not about to break your door in. I'm here to talk about Ben and what he did, breaking into my brother's place, putting a gun to my mother's head and terrorizing the little girl my brother and his wife are adopting. Do you have any idea what that kind of event does to a kid?"

She didn't pull her gaze from him at first, but then she shut her eyes, shaking her head. "Look, as I said, Ben was always a hothead. We never expected him to do what he did. This was about getting Dad out. I suppose you already exacted your revenge, killing him and his friend. Of course I'm not okay with him doing what he did. Joel was the one who called me and told me he had gone too far. One of your team talked with my brothers. I have to wonder, though, is that our fate as well? Is that why you're here, Luke, to kill me?"

The way she said it, she wasn't begging for her life. She was so matter of fact as she lifted her hands toward him. "No, I had no idea Ben would drag an innocent child and your mother into it. Do you want me to say I'm sorry? Would that help?" She turned and strode into the living room, over to a small desk by a bookcase in the corner. A red and gold area rug had been tossed over the hardwood floor, and the walls were all dark wood paneling. The house looked restored, likely a hundred years old.

"I want to know why you were at the bar," Luke said. "You said you didn't plan on me, but you had to know we were there. Who gave you the information?"

"What?" she said. "Why does it matter who? It's done, right? Or are you here for some retribution? Come on, Luke. Yes, I broke into your phone when you were sleeping. Was that the plan? There was no plan, but getting all your contacts and everything helped. It was what my brother had asked for. Ben knew what hotel you were in and figured you'd be at the bar. He knew something about your operation before it went down. I was already at the hotel then, because I had checked in two days earlier, but you probably already know that."

He didn't, but he wondered if Jess did.

"I was in town to convince my dad to leave," she said. "He wouldn't, because he said he was supposed to meet with someone from the BBC. You already know his contact didn't show, so here we are. Dad's out, and we seem to have traded my brother's life for his. If I had to go back, would I do something differently? Yes, of course I would. I wouldn't let Ben shoulder all this himself, especially now, seeing that your family was targeted. This wasn't about going after your families. It was about going after each one of you because of what you did."

"So someone tipped off Ben," he said. "Who was it?"

She lifted her hands in confusion as she stepped around her desk. Her laptop was open. "I don't know.

Some contact he said he had. Military, I think. I didn't ask. Is this why you came all the way out here? You called me, Luke, remember? This is kind of overkill. Or is there something else I need to worry about?" Her eyes were soft and sad at the same time.

"You think I'm here to kill you?"

She just shrugged. Anyone else would have been terrified, but she wasn't. "Well, aren't you?"

"No, I'm not a monster. You think I would sleep with you the way I did and then show up and kill you? This is personal, Rosemary."

"For me too. It's no different than you doing what you did to my dad. He was innocent, and you saying you were ordered to do it doesn't make it right. Guess we could go round and round on this, but it won't solve anything. Who's more wrong here? I'm sorry about your mother and the little girl, but I didn't do it, and neither did my other brothers. Nor did we know Ben would do that. I'd like to think it wasn't Ben's plan. You need to ask yourself if you would've done the same thing as him if the roles were reversed."

Her arms were slender, crossed in front of her. He'd expected her to be nervous, but she was anything but. He couldn't help wondering if she really was that naive about her brother. He'd seen the look in Ben's eyes. He was a trained killer. Would he have pulled the trigger? Without hesitation.

"Not that, never a kid," he said. "I've done things I can't take back, but there're lines I won't cross. Bringing a war to my family wasn't okay."

She nodded. "Point taken, and your team members also got their point through to my brothers. The one who tied Martin up in his garage left him there for over twenty-four hours and dislocated his shoulder, by the way. He didn't deserve that. He was in over his head. Joel and Liam, too. We all got it. Our dad is safe. Joel turned over some of his documents, yes, but the other ones your country wants, the ones you'll never get, I know the men who have them—a copy, that is." She lifted her chin to him.

He nodded. "Now, why did I know you were going to say that?"

She shrugged. "Is this where you demand all of it? If you do, the answer is no. Although my dad's free, there's just something about the way all of this went down that makes me think I'll need my own get-out-of-jail-free card, for me and my family. We're not criminals or bad people."

Could he blame her? No. "I would've thought you'd send your dad's information to all the news stations, journalists everywhere."

"Who says I didn't?" was all she said. He realized there was so much more to Rosemary Brooks than he could have realized.

"You know, there could have been something between us, I like to think," he said.

She pulled in a breath and glanced away, uncomfortable.

"So let me ask you something, face to face," he continued. "If it hadn't been me who approached you, if it had been someone else from the team, would you have slept with him, too?"

She pulled her hand over the back of her neck, and he wasn't sure what to make of her expression—raw, real, maybe. Then she shook her head. "Honestly, Luke, I didn't plan on sleeping with you, but there was something about you that had me doing the one thing I never expected to do. At the same time, I never expected you to take my number, either."

She took a step toward him and then another until she was standing right in front of him, and she settled her hand on his chest and stared at it before pulling in another breath and lifting her gaze to him. "It's that chemistry. You feel it still. I know I do. But acting on it is exactly what neither of us should do."

Then she pulled her hand away and took a step back.

Chapter 21

L uke just couldn't help himself.

What was in his best interest and what he wanted had become two different things, and his self-destructive side had been a part of him for so long that he no longer understood what it meant to do the right thing and be normal. He rested his hand over his forehead and let it settle there, taking in the white ceiling and the light of day that drifted in through the window.

The bedroom was done in whites and pinks. He turned his head and took in Rosemary's closed eyes, her brown hair fanned over her pillow, and her soft breathing, which hadn't evened out.

"You okay?" she said.

What was he supposed to say? His family would likely have a few choice words for him if they knew he was sleeping with someone they would consider the enemy.

She ran her hand over his arm. "You were hurt," she said. "What did you do? What happened?"

Her brother had shot him. At the same time, he wondered if she needed to know. "Flesh wound—it's nothing," he said. "Look, this, here, shouldn't have happened."

Again, there was something about touching this woman, kissing her. He was having trouble remembering who had made the first move, how he'd had her against the wall. Her dress and his shirt were downstairs in the living room, the front door was still open, and here he was, solving nothing, just digging himself deeper into something that couldn't be any kind of healthy relationship.

"Right, just like the first time," she said. "But here you are in my bedroom after you've screwed me again. Acting on chemistry isn't the best course of action. You're not a good person, Luke O'Connell, but here you are in my house, in my bed. This is just sex, you know. We can't have a relationship after what happened. You see me as a bad person, and how could I not see you the same way?"

The way she said it had him rolling over onto his side, taking her in. She was complicated, and there was so much about her that he knew, yet he didn't know her at all. "I don't see you as a bad person, Rosemary. As you said, you didn't hold that gun to my family's heads…"

"But you were the one who went in, all military security, and took my dad. It's hard to see you as being on the right end of that when he did nothing wrong, not as far as I'm concerned. But here you are in my bed. What does that say about how blurred the lines have become?" She'd cut him off, giving him everything, lying on her side in a very comfortable bed.

He reached over and brushed her hair back from her forehead, wondering how he could've explained to anyone why he was still there in her bed and not five steps out the front door already. "Can't change what I did. It's what I do, what I signed on for. I don't get to pick and choose. That's the way the military works."

She didn't pull her gaze from him. He could still taste her on him. How could he want her again? "You know, it never worked, my first husband," she said. "We were divorced after the first year. I don't know how to do long-term commitment. So is this it? We can say goodbye and not see each other again? It would probably be best. My brothers wouldn't understand this."

How could he answer that? "You think my family would be on board? As you said about long-term commitment, I'm the poster child for how a relationship can't work. Does this have to have a label? I like you a lot…" His phone rang from the pocket of his pants on the floor. "Hold that thought," he said, then slid from bed naked and reached for it, seeing the unidentified caller, knowing it was likely someone from his team. "O'Connell."

In the large dresser mirror, he could see his image, framed by the wing chair near the open window and the white gauze of the curtains that rustled in the breeze.

"It's Jess. Where are you?"

He said nothing for a second as he took in Rosemary, who was now sitting up, holding the sheet over her perfect breasts. "Indiana. So what's up?"

"With the girl?"

He was going to nod. "With Rosemary. She's right here."

"She wasn't the source of the info," Jess said. "She wasn't tipped off. It was the brother."

He had already figured that out. Rosemary didn't pull her gaze from him. "I know," he said. "So who told him?"

"Seems it was a commanding officer of the platoon Ben was assigned to. But there's more." He heard the sigh on the other end.

"There always is," he replied.

"Nothing will come back on Sienna," Jess said, and his tone had Luke's stomach pitching and his anger rising.

"So you're saying her hands are clean?"

"I'm saying she knows we're looking," Jess replied. "Rex has already tracked an encrypted message that she sent to Ben Schwartz with dates, times, and our identities."

From the way Rosemary was watching him, she likely had some idea of what he was talking about.

"So my family and what happened…"

"My guess? All Sienna," Jess said.

Luke let the phone slip from his ear as he turned to the window. "And she gets away with it?"

"For now," Jess said. "So what are you doing about the girl?"

Luke knew his team leader had likely already figured out what he was doing. "I'll be heading back tomorrow," he said. He knew Jess understood that he wasn't about to answer.

"Fine, got it. See you on base," he said, then hung up.

Luke took a second as he tossed his cell phone on the chair by the window.

"So you're planning on spending the night?" Rosemary asked.

"Unless you tell me otherwise."

There it was, the hint of a smile. "Did you miss the part about how I suck at relationships?" she said.

He took a step toward the bed and took in this woman, sexy and mysterious. Something about her seemed so much like him in some ways. "Only if you missed the part about us team guys writing the book on how a relationship can't work."

She slid back the sheet. "Well, then I guess this isn't a relationship, just a guy and a girl, and we'll see where it goes."

He grunted, then leaned down on the bed and pressed a kiss to her lips. He pulled back. "Sounds like the perfect arrangement to me."

Turn the page for a sneak peek of
THE HOMETOWN HERO the next book in *THE O'CONNELLS*
Available in print, eBook & audio

The Hometown Hero

In this shocking O'Connell family novel, a brother's secret is exposed, opening up old wounds and creating a scandal that could rock the community.

Big brother Owen O'Connell was only sixteen when his father mysteriously disappeared, forcing him to become a father figure to his five younger siblings. If you were to ask them, they'd say Owen is the perfect older brother with the perfect life: He's single, a plumber, working his own hours in a close-knit community. Owen, though, knows that appearances are often deceiving.

When he is called to a plumbing emergency at the local high school after a grad prank goes wrong, he finds his old rival Tessa Brooks, now a teacher, holding a broken pipe in the middle of the flood, thinking she can fix the problem. However, the two soon make a horrifying discovery: the body of a student tucked away in a closet.

The event brings authorities flocking in, and in the

ensuing chaos, Owen realizes that someone knows too much about his family. Having carefully held the family together since his father disappeared, he is determined to keep their secrets right where they are, dead and buried. But sometimes, secrets get revealed in the most scandalous of ways.

Owen O'Connell, eldest of six, couldn't remember what it was like not to have responsibility resting upon his now broad shoulders. He couldn't remember a time when he didn't have an eye on his younger siblings, worried about something they'd done or could do, or something that could come after any one of them. Even though everyone was grown now, with their own lives, he still felt that kind of responsibility. Though it hadn't been his choice, he couldn't shake the incessant need to know what was going on with his three brothers and two sisters, considering they all found their way into their own brands of trouble. The biggest lesson of all, which he'd learned long ago, was not to share anything with anyone about his life or his family's.

He took in his home workshop, a shed at the back of his two-bedroom bungalow at the edge of town. The cottage to his right was owned by an old woman in her nineties, now in a nursing home, whose grandson had been considerate enough to move in and share his love of hip-hop with the entire neighborhood every night after midnight. The place on the left was a rundown rental with three feet of perpetually overgrown grass, but at least they were quiet.

In the back of his van, he took in the box of elbow PVC pipes he'd just bought to replenish his supply. The van was faded, older. It was missing his company name, O'Connell's Plumbing, but considering he didn't need to drum up business, as most everyone knew who he was, a company decal would've been wasted dollars. If anything, Owen was the one O'Connell who couldn't and wouldn't part with one dime unnecessarily.

He spotted the ancient rusty Datsun as it pulled up and parked behind his van. The engine purred before it shut off, and the squeal of the car door revealed Lori Kramer, slender and five foot five, with sandy blond hair that stopped at her shoulders. Her pretty face still bore the pissed-off expression that had been there since their fight outside the diner where she worked as a waitress. Their on again, off again relationship, which was non-committal and, as far as he was concerned, had no strings attached, no longer worked for her. So what had she done but demand he figure his shit out, as if he were the one who had issues? He didn't, he told himself, but those had pretty much been her exact words: his issues, his lack of commitment.

Finally, because he could feel her drawing closer and hear her flip-flops on the pavement, he was forced to lift his gaze, taking in the godawful mustard dress uniform from the diner and the small box she was carrying. He put down a pipe, wiped his hands on a damp cloth, and gave her everything, seeing the spark in her brown eyes, the light freckles over the bridge of her nose. She dumped the small box on the workbench beside him, and he took in some things of his: a shirt, a toothbrush, some old tools he'd used while fixing her sink, and a watch he hadn't missed. He wasn't sure what else was in there. When he lifted his gaze to her, she didn't say anything for another second.

"Your things." She gestured rather forcefully.

He lifted the old shirt, which he'd forgotten about, and said nothing, taking in everything in the box. He wasn't too inclined to respond.

"You know, I asked you to pick up your things," she said. "Since I didn't hear from you, here I am, driving them out to you. This is just one more reason we're not together, Owen. I can't get you to actually be part of a relationship, to show up, to follow through on anything. You want me only when you want me…"

He let out a rough sigh, knowing she was about to go on and on to fill the silence, something she always did. There was a point he stopped listening and a point at which he was just done, like now.

"I get it," he said. "Apologies. Sorry you had to make the trip over. Anything else?" He rested his hand on the box and took in her face, her lips, which he'd kissed so many times. He liked her, but even now, this situation seemed to be heading fast to confrontation, all because of her need to argue, to push, to get him to… what? Be serious about her when his focus was every-where else.

As she'd so explicitly put it, she wanted the kind of commitment he could never see in their relationship.

"That's it? That's all I get?' She gestured between them quite dramatically. What the hell did she want from him?

He laughed. "Jesus Christ, Lori, what the fuck is this? We're over. You've said your piece already—repeatedly. I get it. You don't need to hammer it to death, if that's what this is. This isn't working. Sometimes things don't. That's life. Again, thanks for bringing my stuff, but I've got nothing else for you. Not sure what you want me to say."

He knew he sounded like an asshole, but he just rested his forearm on the box and flicked his hand. This was something else she did, push and push when things didn't quite go the way she wanted. He could see she just didn't want to let it go, and her anger seemed to hold her where she was.

"Look, I'm sorry," he said. "Is that what you want to hear from me? I can't feel something just because you want me to. It doesn't work that way. You've made your feelings clear, as I've made mine. I'm not in the same space you are, because of…"

"Yes, because of your family, I know," she snapped. "You're all about the O'Connells. Your nose is in all of their lives. All I wanted was to be included. You spend almost every night with them, but I thought maybe I would get tossed a crumb of what's left of you. You never took me once to meet your family. We weren't there yet. You never came out and said those exact words, but getting you to talk and express any kind of reasonable emotion is beyond me. I started to realize we were never going to get 'there,'" she said, complete with air quotes.

He sighed. "Okay, this has been fun, but I've got work to do, and I'm not rehashing this same old conversation about how you don't understand me. I don't understand you, either, or your need to share everything…" His phone rang, and for a second, he thought the gods were smiling down on him with the interruption. He reached for it, taking in the fact that Lori was still standing there. "I have to take this," he said.

She inclined her head, but she didn't move. Great, so she wanted to take another chunk out of his ass.

He answered and pressed his phone to his ear, giving Lori his back as he took in the rest of his shop. "Yeah? Owen here."

"Owen, this is Rita Mae, down at the high school. We've got ourselves kind of a problem down here, a plumbing emergency. There's water everywhere. It's coming from the second-floor girls' bathroom. We're not sure what happened, but…"

"Okay, on my way. Has anyone shut the main water valve off yet?" He turned around and took in Lori still standing there, her arms crossed, taking in everything he was saying.

"No, custodial is gone for the day. I have a call in to them."

Owen shook his head. "No, look, I'm on my way. I'll be there in less than ten."

He'd shut the main off himself, find out what the problem was, and fix it. At least this was his get-away-from-Lori card, he thought as he hung up and pocketed his phone. He could sense that she just didn't want to let go of this fight. He reached for his keys, giving his shop one last look, but everything he'd need—all the tools and supplies—was already in his van for exactly this reason.

"I have to go, Lori, an emergency call," he said and started walking out of his shop. When she didn't move for a second, he reached up to pull the garage door down, waiting until she finally did. She had realized this was it, and she walked past him and out of the shop.

He pulled down the door and slipped on the lock that would keep out no one who really wanted to get in. Her Datsun was still parked behind his van, and she stopped at her door and took him in. For a minute, he thought she was going to start in on him again. That was just something she did—another reason, he realized, why not seeing her had actually lifted a weight off him. Lori, although fun at times, could be a lot to handle.

"Lori, I'm sorry," he said. "I don't know how many ways I can say it, but it's over. I'm not where you are. I hope you find someone who can give you what you're looking for, but it's not me. You said it, and you were right, so let's just leave it at that."

She opened her mouth as if to say something, but she let out a sigh instead. Evidently, she'd changed her mind. She shook her head, slipped into her vehicle, started the old heap, and pulled away.

And instead of feeling sad at the ending of their relationship, he felt relieved.

The Hometown Hero, Chapter 2

Owen took in the local high school and the few teens in the parking lot, because school was now out for the day. He remembered the concrete institution fondly, but he thought that was mostly nostalgia, because it was also a reminder that for him and his siblings, school hadn't been a happy social time. Today, if you asked him, he wouldn't be able to recall any of the fundamental knowledge that had been crammed into them back then.

He pulled his tool kit from the van, looping the strap over his shoulder. In just his faded blue T-shirt, he felt the chill in the air as he pulled out his phone and saw Karen's text: *Can you pick up some wine on your way over? Jack and I have to meet with a client and are running late.*

Right, everyone was going to Marcus and Charlotte's new house, which they'd just signed the papers on, across from Ryan and Jenny's. At least Marcus was now married, with a baby on the way, and then there was his adoption of Eva. Marcus, out of all of them, was the one who had really pulled his shit together.

Owen strode up the sidewalk, seeing the cracks in the cement and remembering the spot where he'd dropped his history teacher's keys into the freshly poured concrete. Helga Adams had made every day in that class a living hell for him. To this day, he'd never shared with anyone the fact that he was the one who had taken her keys from her desk. Even though she'd accused him, she'd never been able to prove it.

He pulled open the front door and spotted Rita Mae, redheaded and slender, about ten years his senior, coming from the office. Evidently, she'd been waiting for him, as she hurried his way. His sneakers squeaked on the industrial concrete floor, looking right and left to see if anything out there was coming his way—just a habit he couldn't shake.

"Owen, thank goodness you're here," Rita Mae said. "It's quite a mess. There's water everywhere, and I don't know what to make of what happened. You know, every year about this time, I expect those seniors to pull something. When I heard there was water coming down the stairs from the girls' bathroom, I just knew it was them. I hope it's not going to be too bad! It seems the kids are getting more creative every year with their so-called pranks, which are destructive to school property. From the toilet paper decorating the entire hall to Mr. Goodman's motorcycle on the roof of the school last year—though how they got it up there, I have no idea—and now this, something just has to be done with those kids…"

He was following Rita Mae down the hall, and he took in how quiet the place was. "So, speaking of misfits, where're all the kids?" he added as he started up the stairs. "Seems rather quiet, considering."

"You're right," she said. "School's out for the day, and we don't see many sticking around, maybe a few here and there. It's amazing, though. Today it's absolutely deserted, which tells me every kid in the school likely knew this was going to happen and skedaddled instead of having to answer questions and face the music. What is it with teenagers?"

He wondered whether she expected him to answer. He took in the water on the stairs, a thin stream. As his feet splashed through the puddles, he realized Rita Mae was still talking, carrying on about the seniors. He knew well those kinds of pranks, that kind of trouble. The O'Connells had been neck deep in it at one time.

Marcus had been the worst. Any time trouble happened at school, nine times out of ten, Marcus had been behind it, had known about it, or had been a part of it. Then there was Ryan. Owen had lost count of the number of times he'd pulled his younger brothers out of something: doing graffiti, keying the principal's car, letting air out of the science teacher's tires… His other younger brother, Luke, had pretty much taken care of himself. Karen was one he'd had to watch extra closely, and then there was Suzanne, who had always given the impression that everything was fine even when it wasn't. Now look at them. He wondered if he'd ever be able to shake his need to herd them all, to keep tabs on all of them.

As he topped the stairs, he spotted the sheen of water coming from the bathroom just ahead, where the door was open. He found himself looking at the concrete block walls, the girls' sign on the open door.

Rita Mae went in first and peered around the

corner. "Owen is here now. OMG, look at you, girl! This mess…"

He wasn't sure whom she was talking to at first, but as he stepped into the bathroom, he saw her: her blond hair pulled back into a neat bun, her slender curves in navy slacks and a white tank top, her flat shoes in the water on the floor. The paneling had been pulled off the wall that led to the plumbing, and he could see the wrench in her hand. She was reaching as high as she could on tiptoes to bang the red valve, which he knew was the water shut-off.

She turned her head. All the while, water was still spraying out from what he could now see was a busted pipe. For a second, he felt shocked, looking into her face, oval perfection. Her white tank left nothing to the imagination, soaked. She could've won a wet T-shirt contest, as it was practically sheer over her perfect breasts. He had to remind himself this was Tessa Brooks, his first crush, though that had crashed and burned, and she was now just an old rival.

Right. Someone had mentioned long ago that she was now a teacher.

"Well, are you going to do something, or are you going to just stand there and keep staring at my breasts?" she said, then made a rude noise. He thought she'd dropped the F-bomb under her breath. Right, she also had a smart mouth. He'd forgotten about that.

She turned back around and gripped the wrench, about to swing it and pound away at the red lever again, so he reached out and grabbed her wrist, holding it just as she went to swing again. It was that damn competitive drive, as if she thought she could do everything better than him.

"Whoa, what the hell, Tessa? Stop before you break something." He went to take the wrench, but she seemed to grip it harder, giving him everything in that one look. He was still holding her wrist, but he didn't let go, just stepped in right beside her. She was tall and slender, with perfect curves, about five inches shorter than him. *Pull it together, Owen.* Her eyes were blue, vivid, and flashing with hellfire—and then there were those lips.

"Take your hands off me," she said, enunciating each word carefully through gritted teeth so there was no chance he'd misunderstand.

Water was still spraying out, soaking his shirt now too, and what did he do but put his other hand on the wrench to pry it from her? He tossed it onto the floor in the water, then somehow maneuvered her back and reached up to shut off the water. The spray stopped, and the water slowly drizzled and then dripped.

"It was one hand, Tessa," he said. "Now that I'm here, you can let a professional fix this before you break something and turn what'll likely be a simple fix into something far more costly and time-consuming."

She didn't pull those magnificent blue eyes from him. She could tell him to fuck off with just a look, and he could see she was likely thinking of a way to tell him how she could and would do things better than he would.

"I was trying to turn the water off and almost had it, Owen."

He knew she hated him. At the same time, everything about her brought up unsettling and frustrating feelings inside him. He took in the counter, seeing the gray duct tape, and he reached for it and lifted it. Rita

Mae had evidently realized she was in the middle of something personal and had quietly stepped out.

"You planning on doing something with this?" Owen said, tossing the duct tape back on the wet counter and setting his tool case beside one of the sinks. He took a better look at the busted pipe, wondering what had caused this. He doubted this was a prank. More than likely, from the looks of it, the pipe was just old and had been about to give for some time.

"I was planning on fixing the pipe," she snapped. "I was going to turn the water off and then duct tape it until it could be fixed. You know, I'm not completely useless, Owen. I have two hands and the ability to problem-solve, which was exactly what I was doing. Then here you are, showing up and thinking I'm out of my depth. I'll have you know I had a handle on the situation, and—"

"Are you finished?" He cut her off, facing her.

She was standing there, holding her ground. The woman was infuriating, and he quickly remembered how she never had gone quietly into the night. No, scratch that. She had never sat back and counted on him for anything. As if she had realized how indecent her shirt was, she simply crossed her arms under those amazing breasts and gave him everything.

Confidence. Two can play this game.

"Evidently," she said, then gestured to the tools and the sink. "I'll leave you to this, then."

He had expected something else from her. No, he had *wanted* something else. Her walking away that easily should've been a relief, but there was something about her attitude that he craved. What was it about Tessa? He had anticipated fighting with her, sparring with her, because their arguments had been on another level. No other woman could compete.

"So how did this happen?" he added, taking in her confusion as she stepped back. "Rita Mae said it was a school prank, seniors, but these pipes are old, no longer up to code. Corrosion and wear is what this looks like."

He took in the pipes intently only because he was finding it damn difficult to keep his gaze from her. When he reached up for the red shut-off lever, he felt how corroded that was, as well.

"I have no idea," she said. "I was in my classroom, finishing up for the day, and was just about ready to pack it up and leave when something caught my eye. I stepped out of my classroom to investigate and saw water everywhere. I followed it into the bathroom here and found all this…"

As she gestured, someone screamed. In the second that followed, Tessa gave him everything before darting out the door ahead of him. Around the corner, he spotted Rita Mae standing outside a room labeled *Janitor*, staring down at something in shock.

As he stepped behind both women and took in the closet, he realized what the problem was. He was staring at the body of a young man, curled up, unmoving. On pure instinct, he moved both Rita Mae and Tessa aside and crouched down, seeing the lifeless eyes of what looked like a student. He reached in and checked for a pulse, but just looking at him, he already knew he was dead.

About the Author

"Lorhainne Eckhart is one of my go to authors when I want a guaranteed good book. So many twists and turns, but also so much love and such a strong sense of family."

(Lora W., Reviewer)

New York Times & USA Today bestseller Lorhainne Eckhart is best known for her writing Raw Relatable Real Romances, where "Morals and family are running themes. Danger, romance, and a drive to do what is right will see you glued to the page." As one fan calls her, she is the "Queen of the family saga." (aherman) writing "the ups and downs of what goes on within a family but also with some suspense, angst and of course a bit of romance thrown in for good measure." Follow Lorhainne on Bookbub to receive alerts on New Releases and Sales and join her mailing list at LorhainneEckhart.com for her Monday Blog, books news, giveaways and FREE reads. With over 120 books, audiobooks, and multiple series published and available at all retailers now translated into six languages. She is a multiple recipient of the Readers' Favorite Award for Suspense and Romance, and lives in the Pacific Northwest on an island, is the mother of three, her oldest has autism and she is an advocate for never giving up on your dreams.

"Lorhainne Eckhart has this uncanny way of just hitting the spot every time with her books."

(Caroline L., Reviewer)

The O'Connells: *The O'Connells of Livingston, Montana are not your typical family. A riveting collection of stories surrounding the ups and downs of what goes on within a family but also with some suspense, angst and of course a bit of romance thrown in for good measure "I thought I loved the Friessens, but I absolutely adore the O'Connell's. Each and every book has totally different genres of stories but the one thing in common is how she is able to wrap it around the family which is the heart of each story." (C. Logue)*

The Friessens: *An emotional big family romance series, the Friessen family siblings find their relationships tested, lay their hearts on the line, and discover lasting love! "Lorhainne Eckhart is one of my go to authors when I want a guaranteed good book. So many twists and turns, but also so much love and such a strong sense of family." (Lora W., Reviewer)*

The Parker Sisters: *The Parker Sisters are a close-knit family, and like any other family they have their ups and downs. "Eckhart has crafted another intense family drama…The character development is outstanding, and the emotional investment is high…" (Aherman, Reviewer)*

The McCabe Brothers: *Join the five McCabe siblings on their journeys to the dark and dangerous side of love! An intense, exhilarating collection of romantic thrillers you won't want to miss. — "Eckhart has a new series that is definitely worth the read. The queen of the family saga started this series with a spin-off of her wildly successful Friessen series." From a Readers' Favorite award—winning author and "queen of the family saga" (Aherman)*

Billy Jo McCabe Mystery: *The social worker and the cop, an unlikely couple drawn together on a small, secluded Pacific Northwest island where nothing is as it seems. Protecting the innocent comes at a cost, and what seems to be a sleepy, quiet town is anything but.*

Lorhainne loves to hear from her readers! You can connect with me at:
www.LorhainneEckhart.com
lorhainneeckhart.le@gmail.com

facebook.com/AuthorLorhainneEckhart

twitter.com/LEckhart

instagram.com/lorhainneeckhart

bookbub.com/profile/lorhainne-eckhart

pinterest.com/lorhainneeckhart

Also by Lorhainne Eckhart

The Outsider Series

The Forgotten Child (Brad and Emily)

A Baby and a Wedding *(An Outsider Series Short)*

Fallen Hero (Andy, Jed, and Diana)

The Search *(An Outsider Series Short)*

The Awakening (Andy and Laura)

Secrets (Jed and Diana)

Runaway (Andy and Laura)

Overdue *(An Outsider Series Short)*

The Unexpected Storm (Neil and Candy)

The Wedding (Neil and Candy)

The Friessens: A New Beginning

The Deadline (Andy and Laura)

The Price to Love (Neil and Candy)

A Different Kind of Love (Brad and Emily)

A Vow of Love, A Friessen Family Christmas

The Friessens

The Reunion

The Bloodline (Andy & Laura)

The Promise (Diana & Jed)

The Business Plan (Neil & Candy)

Keep Me in Your Heart

The O'Connells

The Neighbor

The Third Call

The Secret Husband

The Quiet Day

The Commitment

The Missing Father

The Hometown Hero

Justice

The Family Secret

The Fallen O'Connell

The Return of the O'Connells

And The She Was Gone

The Stalker

The O'Connell Family Christmas

The Girl Next Door

The McCabe Brothers

Don't Stop Me (Vic)

Don't Catch Me (Chase)

Don't Run From Me (Aaron)

Don't Hide From Me (Luc)

Don't Leave Me (Claudia)

Out of Time

A Billy Jo McCabe Mystery

Nothing As it Seems

Hiding in Plain Sight

The Cold Case

The Trap

Above the Law

The Wilde Brothers

The One (Joe and Margaret)

The Honeymoon, A Wilde Brothers Short

Friendly Fire (Logan and Julia)

Not Quite Married, A Wilde Brothers Short

A Matter of Trust (Ben and Carrie)

The Reckoning, A Wilde Brothers Christmas

Traded (Jake)

Unforgiven (Samuel)

The Holiday Bride

Married in Montana

His Promise

Love's Promise

A Promise of Forever

The Parker Sisters

Thrill of the Chase

The Dating Game

Play Hard to Get

What We Can't Have

Go Your Own Way

A June Wedding

Kate & Walker

One Night

Edge of Night

Last Night

Walk the Right Road Series

The Choice

Lost and Found

Merkaba

Bounty

Blown Away: The Final Chapter

The Saved Series

Saved

Vanished

Captured

Single Titles

He Came Back

Loving Christine

For my German Readers

Die Außenseiter-Reihe

Der Vergessene Junge

Der Gefallene Held

For my French Readers

L'ENFANT OUBLIÉ

www.ingramcontent.com/pod-product-compliance
Lightning Source LLC
Chambersburg PA
CBHW032012180726
48283CB00008B/2641